THE CLEAN-UP

It was not a situation that would appeal to everyone, but ten thousand dollars plus his reluctance to avoid a challenge to his courage and ingenuity made Rush Henry take the job. He didn't know who his client was and was told that he'd never find out, but his instructions were explicit: Clean up Forest City! It sounded like a tough assignment and proved to be even tougher than it sounded. Beau Marr, Max Carney and Card Sully had the city in their pockets. Gambling, prostitution and the most vicious of racketeering flourished, operated almost openly, but Rush could find no chink or crevice in the smooth, powerful organization the Big Three had perfected during their many years of unopposed dominance. Yet somewhere there had to be a weakness where Rush could start blasting. It would mean violence, probably bloodshed and death —but it was a job that had to be done, and it would not be the first time Rush had invited the Grim Reaper to peer over his shoulder.

The Clean-Up

by

JOE BARRY

WILDSIDE PRESS

www.wildsidepress.com

Published simultaneously in the Dominion of Canada by George J. McLeod, Limited, Toronto.

FOR MOM
who should know why

Chapter 1

Rush checked them off in his mind. Tom Macy was in Joliet. Meyer and Dorn were in a Federal clink somewhere. Gaust was dead and so was Vic Covici. Jago was in Joliet and Wilmer—where was Wilmer? He lifted his phone and dialed a number.

A voice answered, "Homicide."

"Carnahan," said Rush.

"Carnahan speaking."

"Rush Henry here. Sam, where is that Wilmer? Remember him? You jugged him on the Germaine thing. I know Jago, his boss, is still in Joliet. Merwin visited his uncle there last month and saw him. I'd like a line on Wilmer, though."

There was a silence on the line while Carnahan spoke to someone on an intercom system. Then his voice in the phone.

"He got ten to twenty. Still has at least six with good behaviour. He was in at last count."

"Thanks, Sam," said Rush.

"Anything we can use?"

"No, I was just checking something." He hung up and looked off into the space beyond his window. That was the list so far as he knew. All present and 'best of all' accounted for. No one else, that he could name, wanted him on a spot badly enough to work at it. He looked back to his desk top and the slip of white paper. It had come in a plain white envelope. The typing was short and to the point.

If you wish to learn something to your advantage come to the corner of Fifty-fifth and Harwood at eight o'clock this evening. Further instructions will be given you at that time.

It was unsigned. His first reaction had been to throw it in the wastebasket so he did, having found that first reactions were usually best. Then he got bored. There was money in the bank in quite respectable sums. Marion Dorr was on vacation and Quinn Cornell was in Florida. Life palled. No one to spend that money on. He had been considering buying himself a vacation when Gertrude, the broad office body who ran Rush Henry, Investigations when Rush was away and almost when he was not, had laid the slip of white paper on his desk. He read it, laughed, tossed it in the wastebasket. Then he leaned back and was bored some more. Finally he reached for the paper, smoothed it out and reread it.

It was so obviously a trap that it couldn't possibly be one. Boredom took the count in one round of sixty seconds. He called Gertrude.

"Get me Merwin. I want him to do some shadowing."

"I didn't know we had a case," said Gertrude.

"We don't."

"Then who's he shadowing, a blonde you met in a bar?"

"No, dear," said Rush with satisfaction, "he is shadowing me."

After careful reconnaissance at Fifty-fifth and Harwood Rush stepped forward to meet fate in the guise of something to his advantage. He stood in plain view on the corner and waited. It was a short wait. A limousine of ancient vintage drew up beside him and a dry brittle voice spoke his name.

"Mr. Henry?"

"Yes," said Rush taking a step toward the car.

The door swung open before him.

"Please get in, Mr. Henry."

Rush crossed his fingers and stepped into the back seat. Not until then did he realize that all curtains were drawn. He hoped Merwin could flag a cab. The crusty voice spoke in the darkness.

"Are you quite sure you were not followed, Mr. Henry?"

Rush peered into the darkness beside him.

"No," he said. "I'm not sure. I wasn't expecting to be so I didn't check."

"Does anyone else know you are here?"

Rush felt it safe to ignore Merwin.

"Not a soul," he said.

"Good," said the dry old voice.

Apparently that was all for now. The limousine moved smoothly through Outer Drive traffic and headed north. They passed the loop and continued on the northern Outer Drive. Through Evanston, Skokie and into Winnetka. There they left the boulevard and traveled east toward the Lake. At last the car turned in a driveway and came to rest under the portico of what seemed to be at least a mansion. A servant opened the door and stood back as Rush left the car. His companion stepped out behind him and in the light shed from the entrance Rush saw that his companion was spryer than his voice had indicated, for he was up the steps ahead of Rush, white hair showing under the back brim of a black homburg. A white scarf edged the top of a black caracul top coat. Rush gathered that he was to follow. The older man led him down a hall and through a door into a pleasant study lined with books. Rush, having worn only a hat, had time to study the books while his host removed his outer garments. They were all law books. He couldn't decide if this surprised him or not.

"His host turned to him.

"Will you have a drink, Mr. Henry?"

"I will, indeed. Rye, if you have it."

The old man turned to the servant who stood in the doorway.

"I believe there is a bottle of the old rye in the

basement, Rogers. Will you bring it, please?"

Rush wondered what "the old rye" might be as he took the chair indicated. His host walked around behind the desk and sat down. He rubbed his hands together briefly, looked down at the desk top as if to refresh his memory from invisible notes and at last looked up to Rush.

"I imagine there are many questions you would like to ask me, Mr. Henry."

Rush felt that was obvious so he sat waiting.

"I'll try and anticipate your questions. First, my name is Leach; Aaron Leach. I am a lawyer associated with the firm of Leach, Carruthers and Leach, of whom you may have heard."

Rush had. They were old line counsellors. Rush would have used the word barrister. Their line was trusts and estate managements, wills and probates, family advisors to the long wealthy. His imagination didn't extend to a picture of what they wanted with him. He still waited.

Mr. Leach took another look at his invisible notes and the servant reentered the room. On a tray he carried two bottles. One Rush recognized as a wine bottle, the other almost took his breath away. Slowly he found himself getting up from his chair and walking across to the taboret on which Rogers had set the tray. He picked up the bottle and stared at it unbelievingly. He fondled the bottle in reverent hands and turned to Leach.

"Where did you get this?"

Leach was only mildly surprised at his question. Rush had the fleeting impression that the older man was prepared to expect anything from a private detective.

"Why, I believe it's part of a case or two I bought a good many years ago. Old Overholt, isn't it?"

"Yes," said Rush in a hushed voice. "It's Old Overholt. Old Overholt, 1855. I thought I had helped drink the last bottle of this west of Pennsylvania."

"That would be at Henry Cornell's. He and I bought a shipment of the stuff in the late nineties sometime. Never cared for it myself." He looked over the rims of his glasses at Rush. "You're about the right age. Henry's daughter, Quinn, must have served it to you."

Rush nodded, his eyes on the bottle.

"Well, pour yourself a drink and sit down. I wish to get to the business at hand."

Rush poured three inches in a highball glass and resumed his seat.

"I'm sure you will understand," said Mr. Leach, "that this is entirely outside the usual course of our affairs. To my knowledge this is the first time my firm has been called upon to retain the services of a private detective."

Rush wondered what calamity brought the call this time.

"I assure you that only a deep sense of loyalty to an old friendship brought me into the affair at all. I may as well tell you that I am acting at the request of a schoolmate of mine, now in practice in another city. Through him I represent one of his clients." Leach got up and poured himself a glass of the wine. Back in his seat behind the desk he sipped like nothing else in the world but a bird billing water from a cup. He savored the wine and then continued. "We were asked to investigate you thoroughly and in the event we found you satisfactory we were to retain your services."

His voice droned on like a DC-3 in the distance where Rush began to wish he was. He wasn't though. He was right there in his chair and short of sheer rudeness Rush couldn't hurry him. He wished he'd get to the point.

"The report from Weston was more than satisfactory. If I may say so, you succeeded admirably with a very difficult task."

You may, thought Rush. You everlastingly may. But who cares about that now. That was four years ago.

"Your record with the military intelligence was, of course, not an open book, but your superior officers have assured me that you were invaluable to them."

Rush wondered how this antique set piece had ever gotten to the Colonel. He wondered what was on his mind. He bet himself another drink of the Overholt that it would involve getting somebody out of trouble.

"Of course I have personal knowledge, through the press of your activities in several instances here in Chicago. They impressed me highly."

It was time, Rush decided, to come to the point.

"Look, Mr. Leach," he said. "I won't try to convince you that my time is valuable. It isn't unless I'm working. But you're a lawyer with a large practice and yours must be. All you've done so far is reconvince yourself that you want me to do something for you. Let me suggest that you try convincing me that I should do it. And as a first step, let me in on what it is you want done."

"Dear me," said the older man, "that's coming right to the point, isn't it?"

"Yes," said Rush.

Mr. Leach ran a bony hand through thinning gray hairs and brought it back to rub his chin.

"You must forgive me, Mr. Henry," he said. "I'm a little out of my usual orbit. The request I have to make of you is a little breathtaking I'm afraid. It has no precedent in my experience and I find it hard to believe that anyone could seriously ask that it be done."

The old man was obviously in deep water. Rush made it easier for him.

"Why don't you bring it out and lay it on the

table? Let me look at this unprecedented what-is-it. Maybe I can tell you if it can be done."

The old man nodded his head slowly as if agreeing on a point at law.

"I suspect that you are right. That would be the wisest course." He took a deep breath. "Briefly," he said, "My client wishes to retain your services to the end that you clean up a city."

"Any particular city?" asked Rush. "Or can I choose my own?"

Mr. Leach looked startled.

"Forget it," said Rush. "I was joking. What city does your client have in mind?"

"I'm not at liberty to tell you that until you accept the commission."

"Okay. Then tell me this. Why does your client feel that his town needs cleaning up?"

Leach thought that one through for a moment.

"Why, the usual reasons. Graft, gambling, racketeering."

"Let me make a point," said Rush. "I am a realist where the running of cities are concerned. I'd have to be convinced that the place really needed a bath. Many a conscientious citizen innocently imagines that a few crap games and a slot machine or two mean that the mayor or the chief of police or both are getting rich. That is seldom the case. Mostly those crap games and slot machines are running because the authorities know the people are going to gamble and they'd rather have it out in the open where they can check it rather than under cover and getting away with murder. I'm afraid I would have to refuse to be the leading edge of a blow struck by a reformer who had been scared by a pair of dice."

"You surprise me," said Mr. Leach when he had digested that. "I hadn't expected to find a political philosopher in the person of a private detective."

"You'll find stranger things than that," promised Rush.

"In regard to your remarks, however," said Mr. Leach. "I have certain facts to pass on that should remove all doubt as to the advisability of cleaning up this city. I am reliably informed that there are in the neighborhood of a hundred permanently established places catering to gamblers and offering all types of games of chance. There are protective associations for every type of merchant, retail or wholesale, with standard rates for non-existent services. There are no figures on the profession called the oldest but its practitioners are numerous and available in all grades."

He paused and looked at Rush as if to ask if that were enough.

"Dope?" asked Rush.

"So I am told."

"Okay," Rush said. "It sounds like a nice operation. It should be a pleasure to kick it over. Who is offering how much to get the job done?"

"I can only tell you half of that," said the older man. "Your employer must remain anonymous. As a matter of actual fact I haven't the faintest idea as to his identity myself. As I told you I was brought into the affair by an attorney in the city in question who asked that I investigate you. Your exploits in Weston had come to his client's attention and seemed to indicate that you were the man for the job."

"I'm not sure I like that," said Rush. "But how much is he offering?"

"Ten thousand dollars plus unlimited expenses."

Rush lit a cigarette and blew smoke at the ceiling.

"That's a lot of money. Those unlimited expenses are liable to run high. It seems like a fairly sizeable wad for a citizen to blow on public spirit. Are you sure there isn't a gimmick in it somewhere?"

"Gimmick?" asked Leach.

"A catch. The people who will put up that kind of money just out of civic pride can be counted on the fingers of one finger. Your unknown client must have an angle. I'd like to know what it is."

"I was told you'd ask that question."

"Were you given an answer?"

"I was. My client had a son just past twenty-one but holding a responsible job. Rather large sums of money were available to him. Other people's money, I should say. He managed to lose considerable amounts of it and, I am told, owed even more. He was found dead in circumstances that suggested suicide. The police called it that and there the matter rests. My client doubts it a little since he is very wealthy and could have refunded the money had it been brought to his attention."

"Does he want me to dig the truth about that?"

Leach shook his head.

"No. He feels that the general evil is responsible rather than any individual and he wants the whole thing pulled out by the roots."

"A large order," said Rush. "A very large order. I wonder if he has any idea what it involves."

"I'm sure I couldn't say."

"I'll tell you. It means a dirty, messy, and probably bloody war. People will get hurt and some of them will be innocent bystanders whose worst offense was probably swearing on Sunday. Mr. X will probably get his belly full before I'm half through but tell him from me to grit his teeth and take it because once I get started I'm not going to stop."

"You'll accept then?"

Rush realized that he had already mentally taken on the job.

"Yes," he said, "I'll make a stab at it. Are you sure it's wise for me to have no way to get to Mr. X?"

"That's the way he wants it."

"It should be an easy thing for a detective to run him down through his son," said Rush.

Leach smiled faintly.

"I'm told that one of the few advantages of a setup such as exists in this city is that money can buy anything and Mr. X has a great deal of money. I'm under the impression that no one suspects that his son's death was anything but natural."

"So be it," said Rush. "Now, what's the name of this sinful city?"

"Forest City. Do you know it?"

Rush shook his head.

"No," he said. "I don't know it. I know where it is though and I rather suspect that I'll get to know it quite well."

Leach rose from his seat with obvious relief.

"I'm glad this is out of my hands now," he said. "It isn't at all the kind of thing I like to handle."

Rush grinned.

"I can imagine," he said. "There's one other thing. Am I to go it blind or will X give me some background information? I'd like to know who runs what and who works for who, also where do I get expense money? I expect to need a lot of it."

"A letter will be delivered to you in Forest City with a complete history of the setup there with names and spheres of influence. As to expenses, five thousand dollars will be deposited to any name you wish at the First National Bank of Forest City.

When you are through you may call on me for your fee."

"Satisfactory," said Rush. "Eminently satisfactory. Just tell him to deposit it to the account of Rush Henry. I'm quite fond of my own name and it gives me one less thing to remember."

Leach led him to the door of the study and opened it. Down the hall at the outer door an argument was in progress. A voice raised clear and strong in the confines of the hall.

"I'm comin' in if I hafta blast my way in. He's in there. I saw him go in."

Rush recognized the voice. He turned to Leach.

"You'll have to excuse this. That is Wilmer. He's my man. I had him follow me in case your letter was a trap of some sort. I'm afraid he's gone a little overboard in his anxiety about me."

"Think nothing of it," said Leach. "I think it indicates a note of caution that I won't have to give you myself. You seem prepared to take care of yourself."

"Yes," said Rush. "I can take care of myself."

He wasn't thinking of himself, however, as he hurried down the hall toward Merwin. He was thinking of the innocent bystanders.

Chapter 2

"Why all the mystery?" asked Pappy Daley.

"There you've got me. He got me to his house in such a way that I expected to meet emissaries of some foreign power. It was straight out of E. Phillips Oppenheim. So, as a matter of fact, was he."

Pappy looked at Rush through a blue haze of cigar smoke. He added up the chances of success for Rush. He'd known him ten years—five of them as a member of his reportorial staff on the *Express*. He looked at the sum and decided that if he wanted a city cleaned up he'd call on Rush Henry. He said as much.

"Thank you, Pappy," said Rush. "Now, can you do me a little concrete good? I need to know something about Forest City. What can you get me?"

"It just happens that I can. Smoky grew up not ten miles from there in a place called Walker's Landing. It's on a river. I'll get him."

He lifted a phone and asked for Smoky. Somebody found him in a bar and fifteen minutes later he was in Pappy's office.

"Forest City?" He put a pair of well fatted fingers to his nose. "It stinks. I worked a summer there for Bill Prime on the *Chronicle* when I was drying myself behind the ears. They're organized there."

"Who's organized there?" asked Rush.

"I don't remember the names. There's two or three of them. But they have things split up and greased like you never saw before."

"No kickback from the public?"

"Hell, they've got things so well organized that the public doesn't even know they're there. Sure they've got gambling and they know it. But they don't think it's really harmful, 'people will gamble, you know.' They know that some of the merchants pay off a little but it doesn't come out of their pockets so what the hell. Everything works nicely and there's no crime that anybody can find, so they keep on electing the same guys. It's a gravy train. The guys running the place are in it for the long haul so they aren't trying to get rich over night. It's a tight little setup that nobody can put a finger on and nobody can break."

"Nobody?" asked Rush.

Smoky started to repeat "nobody" when he caught the tone of Rush's voice. He looked at him carefully. Then he took a deep breath.

"You," he said. It was more statement than question.

Rush nodded.

Smoky groaned.

"Here we go again. Look, chum, if you think

Weston was a chore, wait till you hit Forest City. Weston was a dream compared to that spot. You had factions to push around in Weston. In Forest City they got cooperation. Nobody is after anything anybody else has got unless it is J. Q. Public. You've got no edge in Forest City. If you're asking me, which I know damn well you won't, keep your hands off. That's a closed corporation."

Rush grinned at him.

"When I need some help I'll phone you, Smoky. You'll love it. In the meantime what was the name of that publisher in Forest City?"

"Bill Prime."

"Is he honest?"

"He was. He was smart, too. He knew what was going on but he knew he couldn't do anything about it, so he stood clear of it."

"Maybe I can needle him into it. If he's still honest."

"Don't tell him you know me. I got him sued for slander. I was just a growing boy and I managed to forget a comma at the last minute and somebody sued him. It was brutal. That's when I came to work in Chicago."

"You still don't know about commas," said Pappy.

"No, but you've got big time proof readers."

Rush stood up then.

"I've got to go. I'm catching a plane for this

modern Gomorah in an hour. Have Smoky loose when I call. You might send Joe for pix. If I can blow this one up it ought to be good."

At the door he turned back into the room.

"Tell the boys in the back room to have one on me and if I don't come back turn down an empty glass."

An hour later Rush leaned back in his plane seat and opened the envelope Gertrude had handed him during his quick trip to his office on the way to the airport. In a matter of seconds he was so engrossed in the data she had gathered that they were airborne before he realized it. The vital statistics on Forest City were interesting but not amazing. Two hundred plus thousand citizens called it home. It was basically an industrial city, manufacturing among other things a vacuum cleaner, a truck and a popularly priced line of furniture. There were three golf courses, seven parks, four municipal swimming pools, and a zoo. The only newspaper was the *Chronicle*, publishing both morning and evening editions. Listed as Mayor was one Patrick Gunn. A Mark Carver was Police Commissioner with a Mr. Thomas Hacker as his Chief of Police.

That was all. Forest City hadn't made much of a mark in the recorded annals of the outside world. From his figures it could have been any one of a hundred other American cities. Rush glanced briefly back through the notes then tore them into very small pieces and put them in the ashtray inset in the arm of his seat. He leaned back and closed his eyes. He was sound asleep when the wheels touched the runway at Forest City's municipal airport.

A cab took Rush through the pleasant tree lined streets that had given the city its name to the heart of town. It was just after five o'clock and the rush was on. He watched as uniformed policemen skillfully handled the heavy flow of traffic and wondered. The first sign of laxness in a police department usually shows in the lowly harness bull. He is a politician first and a policeman when he feels like it. His main interest in life is keeping the right guys in office so that he can keep his job. The policemen Rush saw now were not of this breed. They were nattily uniformed in blue breeches with a wide white stripe and high boots. They were young and confident. They knew their job. Rush wondered if he were in the wrong city.

His driver maneuvered to the curb in front of a hotel whose sign named it the Carter. A doorman helped him out of the cab and a bellhop carried his bag into the lobby. It was more than adequate, it was in fact a very nice hotel. He registered and the clerk handed the bellhop the key to 715. The hop performed the usual ritual of opening a window an inch, lighting the lights in the bathroom, and opening the door to the closet. Rush flipped him a quarter.

"Anything else?" he asked.

"What would you suggest?" asked Rush.

"That depends on what you want," said the bell-hop.

"Entertainment," said Rush. "I'll be here a week or ten days and I want something to kill time."

"Blonde, brunette or redhead?" asked the hop.

"Just like that, huh?"

The bellhop snapped his fingers.

"Just like that. We got a million of 'em."

"I'll make a note of it," said Rush. "I usually like to pick my own women though. How about an extra dollar I might hold. Can I make it grow?"

The bellhop looked at him oddly.

"You are new here aren't you?"

Rush nodded.

"Well, man, you can risk a dollar in every joint in town. This is the gamblingest place you ever saw."

"Got any recommendations?"

"Sure. I'm an honest boy just trying to get along. It'll be worth a fast buck to me if you go to Carlo's and tell them I sent you."

"You'll get the buck," said Rush. "I'll make it tonight."

The bellhop left then and Rush unpacked his bag. He picked up the telephone directory and looked through the classified section. He counted two hundred and some bars, taverns, and night-clubs which made it about one per thousand population. Besides being a gambling town this must also be quite a city for entertainment.

The lobby clock gave the time as six o'clock as he crossed it to the street door and walked down the main street. He walked slowly, taking in the flavor of the town. Several times he stopped in a bar or cocktail lounge for a drink and each time found the inevitable Bingo table, nearly always punchboards on the bar and always at the back of the room were a bank of slot machines handling all denominations of silver coin up to a half dollar. He wasted forty dollars in one of the half dollar machines. It paid ten once, five twice, and two four times. He wondered if all the gambling in town was rigged to the same percentage. It didn't seem likely. They wouldn't get much play after very little of that.

Seven o'clock found him in front of a restaurant built on rather lavish lines with a cocktail bar and floor shows advertised at ten, twelve and two. The inner man rang a gong and he turned in the door. The cocktail bar, a tricky arrangement, down two steps from the level of the restaurant proper was too tempting to miss. Rush straddled a stool and ordered rye in an old fashioned. As it came a soft voice at his shoulder spoke to the bartender.

"Another of the same, Tommy."

Rush turned his head to find red hair flaming

down a bare back turned full in his direction. Below the hair an evening gown of a brilliant green poured in the direction of the floor. A white arm rested its elbow on the bar. As he looked the elbow left the bar and the head came slowly around to look him full in the face. Eyes as green as the dress looked directly into his. There was a nose, faintly tilted which Rush missed as he looked into the eyes. There were also lips—full and red with a humorous twist in the corners. The eyes slanted a little and the mouth said:

"Hello."

Rush took a deep breath and grinned.

"That," he said, "is the neatest trick of the week."

The mouth smiled.

"I thought you'd like it."

"I do. I like it very much. I doubt, though, if very many women could get away with it. You've got a lot, but you need it all for that approach."

"I think you're pretty, too."

Her drink came then and she sipped it, looking over the rim at Rush. The amber in the glass doing strange and wonderful things to her eyes. Rush drained his glass and turned to the bartender.

"Two more of the same, Tommy," he said.

Rush lit a cigarette and puffed a cloud at the ceiling.

"Look," he said. "Let us say that I know the rules of the game. Let us also say that while my intentions may not be strictly honorable that I am easily handled. Now. How firmly are you tied to this joint?"

Her eyes stated all the question necessary.

"I mean, do you have to stay here all evening and if so when are you through, and can I meet you then?"

"Yes, four o'clock, and no."

Rush checked those off.

"You do have to stay here. You're through at four and I can't meet you then."

She nodded over the rim of her glass.

"Okay. Is that last 'no' a final one? There's always Thursday and Friday and all those other days."

She shook her head.

"Quit being mysterious and feminine. What does that mean?"

"It means that the no is not final and yes, there are other days. Everybody knows that."

"I'm glad you're one of them. Tell me something else. Are all the other business girls in town in your class?"

She smiled and it lit a very pleasant light in the green eyes. Then she shook her head. No.

It appeared that the rules didn't bar eating dinner with a customer. In ·fact they encouraged it. So Rush bought a pair of steaks. Over coffee he looked across at the girl whose name was Gay Wimberly.

"Look," he said. "I have quite a few things I have to do this evening so you lose me from here on out."

"I wonder if I'll live," she said.

"You will," said Rush, "because I will be back. You'll find yourself stumbling over me. Plan on it."

He left then and walked along the main street till he found a cruising cab. He hailed it and asked to be taken to Carlo's.

"The M Club is better, buddy," said the cabbie.

"That's nice," said Rush and settled back in his seat.

"Still want to go to Carlo's?"

"Yes," said Rush.

The cab started with a jerk and whirled around a corner. It was only a ten minute ride just past one end of the business district to Carlo's. He paid his driver and walked through the door into a Hollywood set. A man in a Tuxedo met him in the lobby and inquired if he had a reservation.

"I'm not eating," said Rush. "I'm gambling. A hop in the Carter sent me."

It seemed to be standard procedure.

"Of course. You'll find the game rooms at the end of this corridor." He pointed to a wide door on his right.

Rush walked down the short hall and into another cinema set. He had cast lots of odd dollars in casinos from Reno to Florida but this had them beat. Everything was mahogany, or chromium, or leather. It all gleamed richly. A small service bar was placed against one wall and Rush instinctively headed for it. He wanted a moment for orientation. Over his glass of rye he counted four roulette wheels, all doing a good business, four crap tables, half a dozen blackjack dealers with a sprinkling of chuckaluck cages. There were slot machines and even these were in the Hollywood tradition, gleaming like a roadhouse jukebox.

His drink done Rush decided to risk a dollar on the dice. He bought chips at a cashier's cage and elbowed his way into the rim of a table. He watched the roll for a minute or two then tossed five dollars on the come strip. The dice gave him five for a point. Across the table he saw a brief movement and noted a man leaving the table quite hurriedly. Something familiar in the set of the retreating shoulders made him back away for a moment and follow the man with his eyes. He got a sight of the profile for an instant and his memory clicked. It was Sam Percy of the Chicago Percys. Sam dealt in various powdered products whose sale was considered highly illegal by the federal law. Rush grinned at his speedy departure and turned back to the table. It had been some time since one glimpse of his face had sent anyone hightailing it in exactly that way. Well, the horn was blown now. Somebody would know he was in town inside of ten minutes. He looked down at the table. A stack of bills were resting where his five had been. He looked at the dealer.

"Pull down, buddy," said the dealer. "Limit's a hundred on this table."

"What happened?" asked Rush.

"He made your five and four elevens in a row."

Rush took sixty dollars of his pile, leaving a hundred to bet. The dice came out on nine. The line point appeared to be six and the thrower couldn't come close. He rolled a five, an eight, a ten and a four. The sidebet money on the come strip piled high. Watching the stickman rake in the dice, pick them up and toss them to the shooter, Rush caught a flicker of movement that didn't belong. He didn't watch the shooter he watched the dealer for an instant, and as the dice rolled he saw him put a pair of dice in the box in front of him. Then a groan told Rush what the roll had been. A seven. He got it then. He pushed back out of the crowd and strolled to the bar.

It had been the simplest of riggings, yet one of the most effective. If the stickman is expert enough it will make a lot of money for the house. With a pair of honest dice the thrower builds up a lot of money on the line and on the come strip in sidebets. If he keeps shooting without a seven he's going to make a side point for several betters and eventually his front line point. When there is enough money bet to make it worthwhile the stick man drops in a pair of ringers loaded or shaved to roll seven. That wins all bets for the house. Another neat trick, thought Rush. He ordered a double rye.

As he got it halfway to his lips he heard voices raised at the nearest roulette table. He drained his drink and moved closer to catch the argument. A red faced man was insisting to the croupier that he had had a hundred dollar chip on eighteen. The ball had dropped into eighteen and his chip had turned up on fifteen, one square nearer the wheel. He insisted that the croupier's stick had moved it. Rush figured the odds that he was right were about twenty to one. He wondered what would be done about it. He found out immediately. From a door in one side of the room two men moved purposefully toward the table. Rush figured that they had gotten a signal from a foot button pushed by the croupier. They converged on the red faced man and ten seconds later had him out of another side door without his feet having touched the ground. Rush looked at the door as it closed and realized that it opened onto an alley. Swiftly, yet without seeming to hurry, he got his hat and left the building. He turned away from the alley and walked to the opposite corner of the building. A narrow passageway ran toward the rear. He looked around and seeing no one in sight, ducked into the passageway running noiselessly to the back of the building. At the back corner, he paused and listened. He could hear heavy breathing broken by dull thuds. He poked a cautious head around the corner and in the dim light he could see the two men administering a solid beating to the man with the red face. As he looked a fist lashed out catching the man on the point of the chin. He crumpled to a limp heap on the ground. A gruff voice spoke in the gloom.

"Pour some whiskey on him, Charley, while I get a car."

Rush left then. There was nothing he could do for the red faced man. He'd turn up in police court tomorrow morning and pay a fine for drunkenness. Nobody'd ever believe his story, least of all a judge who didn't want to.

Rush caught a cab to the Carter. It had been a long day and bed was very inviting. So inviting in fact that he had his coat half off as he walked through the door into his hotel room. He stopped in mid-motion and slowly shrugged his coat back on. Then he went slowly to his bed and sat on one edge.

"I hope you don't mind if I look over your shoulder," he said to the man who was calmly searching his suitcase.

Chapter 3

"Not at all," said the man and continued his methodical search.

Rush watched him with interest. He finished the suitcase and continued to a briefcase on the dresser. He finished off with a quick once over of the drawers of the dresser and the clothes that Rush had hung in the closets. When he was through he walked to the door and turned with his hand on the knob.

"Thanks," he said and turned the knob.

"Just a moment, old boy," said Rush. "You're not going off without some kind of explanation, are you? I don't think I could stand the strain of the curiosity."

"Yes," said the man.

"There are such things as police," said Rush. "I'd love to have them in. They're always interesting."

"Aren't they?"

"Very. Would you mind talking things over with them?" Rush reached a hand for the bedside phone.

"That won't be necessary," said the man pointing a finger at the phone. "You've got all the law you need right here in the room." He reached in a vest pocket and drew out a shield which he showed to Rush.

"This is very interesting," said Rush. "Is it a courtesy you extend to every visitor to Forest City?"

"Only to private dicks. We don't like them and when they show here we like to know what they are doing."

"Do you know now?"

"No, but we will."

"Would it help if I told you?"

The man turned back into the room.

"I'll listen," he said. "I'll check everything, but I'll listen first. What are you doing here?"

"This will amaze you," said Rush. "Before I got to be a private detective I was a reporter. I'm here on an assignment. I'm doing a series of articles for a Chicago Newspaper on Forest City."

"A reporter? That's worse. We hate reporters."

"I'm quite harmless as a reporter," said Rush.

"What paper?"

"*Express.* I used to work for them."

"Why articles on Forest City?"

"I never thought to ask." Rush looked at his hands. "Is there anything special I should look for?"

The man looked at him carefully for a minute.

"No," he said. "But there are some things you should not look for. And if you start looking for them, you'll find yourself in some important trouble. We don't like snoopers."

"You made that very clear. I'll try hard not to snoop."

The man walked to the door.

"Whom do I have to thank for this visit?" asked Rush.

"I'm Detective Lieutenant Marks," the man said and opened the door.

"You're not leaving?" said Rush. "I have a lot of questions I'd like to ask."

"No," said the man and disappeared through the door. His head reappeared an instant later. "If this article gag is a phony, let me tell you one other thing. We don't have a private eye in the city. We don't issue them licenses, and your Chicago license is no good here. So no investigating. Here you're just another guy named Joe, and we don't like you." This time he was gone for good.

Rush spent no time mourning his unpopularity. He went to bed. There he lit a cigarette and puffed smoke into the gloom. It hung in a cloud pierced by a dim square of light from the window. In the square he saw Weston. Weston with a thin skin of respectability covering rank, festering sores. He had ripped off the skin and performed surgery on the sores cutting them out with precision, leaving the city scarred but clean and whole. Forest City swam into the square. It had a skin, too, but thicker and covering deeper sores of longer standing. It was a new problem. In Weston he had had an edge. His own history had coincided in part with the city. There he had known people, had had a precise picture of who was who and owned what. There there were factions to pit against other factions. It was a simple matter of lighting a new fire under an already boiling pot. There were no factions in Forest City, no boiling pot. It was, as Smoky had said, a closed corporation running smoothly. It required different tactics. He'd have to make a few factions of his own. He was asleep before he decided how.

The Forest City *Chronicle* was housed in a modern building that might have been any office building if it hadn't been for the large plate glass windows overlooking a section of the presses. Rush entered the main door and asked for Mr. Prime. Mr. Prime it appeared was not yet in his office. He asked for back files of the paper and was shown to a room full of back issues of the *Chronicle*. He skimmed them paying attention only to the pages devoted to local news. He learned only one thing. On the record Forest City was as clean of sin as a new born babe. Beyond a few overparking offenses, a little drunkenness and a petty theft too occasional to count, there was nothing. The police of Forest City might well have been on vacation for five years. Nobody did anything criminal. It wasn't alone the fact that nobody had been arrested, there were no complaints. Nobody had required the protection of the poilce or their assistance in solving a crime. It meant only one thing, Rush realized as he left the building. Weston had had a similar arrangement. Other cities had found it to their advantage to make the same deal. For free passage and unmolested shelter, those who lived on the other side of the legal fence paid in kind. They left Forest City free of depredation. No pete man, second story artist, confidence man, stick-up artist, shover of the queer or other practictioner of crime of any sort followed his profession in Forest City. It made for an easy life for cops. It also made for crime waves in varying degrees of violence in neighboring cities.

Rush's passage across the lobby was interrupted by the desk clerk who handed him a thick envelope. He carried it to his room and opened it. It was his promised background information on the organization of Forest City. It was complete, concise, and to the point. An unique document. The first of its sort Rush had ever seen. The covering note was typewritten and unsigned.

In anticipation of your wish and possible attempt to learn my identity I want to make it entirely clear that you will not be able to obtain that knowledge. Beyond that, I ask that you complete your task as quickly as possible and leave the city. Your fee will be waiting for you in Chicago. The expense money you requested is now on deposit at the First National Bank.

The report was as concise:

"First, there are three main divisions ruled by three different men. Max Carney has liquor and rackets, Beau Marr has women and Card Sully has dope. All have gambling. A list of properties owned by each of these men is appended. They are in complete cooperation with each other and are associated in business ventures outside the realm of vice. Each is in a different phase of construction work and no contract is let in Forest Cty without their being given first call. Together they own Mayor Gunn, Commissioner Carver and Chief Hacker body and soul. Through them they operate the city as a private concern. While they do not personally operate every gambling and drinking establishment in the city they oversee them and take a percentage from each operation. All slot machines are the property of Carney. Each has a retinue of followers reminiscent of the gangs in Chicago except that it has not been necessary in many years for a gun to be carried or used. Appended is a list of these men together with the man for whom they work. No figures are available on income but it can be assumed that it is large. There is little friction for the reason that each of the men named above is prospering sufficiently and can look forward to long and continuous success under present circumstances. Money is available in quantities more than sufficient to grease any difficulties."

There was a little more covering interlocking of influences and methods of collection in the matter of percentages and protections. Appended, as promised, were the lists mentioned. Rush folded them and put them under a corner of the rug. The body of the note he read again and then burned, flushing the ashes down the drain in the bathroom bowl.

He went to the window and stared down at the street for a long minute. On the face of it there was no crack, no crevice to insert a chisel and start wrecking. On the face of it, then, he'd have to make his own crack and that looked like dynamite. It took him all of a half hour to decide what kind of dynamite. At the end of the half hour he picked up the phone and placed a call for Pappy Daley at the *Express* office in Chicago. It was through in a pair of minutes.

"Rush talking, Pappy. I need some help."

"Want Smoky to come down?"

"Not yet. I want you to send me some things. Got a pencil?"

"Just a minute. Say. A guy's been in looking for you. Says he wants a job. Just got out of the army."

"What's his name?"

"Twist, Robin Twist."

"The hell. Where is he?"

"At a hotel right now. Who is he?"

"You should remember him, Pappy. He was with me on the Dorn thing. He was in G-2 with me. We worked together most of the time."

"You got a job for him?"

"Any time he wants it. Call him up and tell him he's on the payroll as of right now. Give him some money and ship him down here. I can use him."

"Can do. Any instructions?"

"No. Just tell him to find me without too much fuss. I'm in 715 at the Carter. He'll know how to go about it. Now, have you got the pencil."

"Shoot."

Rush dictated a list of things to Pappy and said good-bye. With the phone in its cradle he looked off into space. Of all the men in the world he could think of no other one he would rather have at his side in the next ten days than Robin Twist. Small, cocky, tough, loyal, and with all the know-how that only Uncle Sam's Military Intelligence can give. He could use the mighty mite, but good. He sighed a major sigh of relief and picked up the phone again. He asked room service to send him a bottle of rye, Old Overholt if available.

Chapter 4

The sun was bright over Forest City's streets as Rush walked through cool morning air to the First National Bank. There was a fresh bite in the air that smelled of early spring or late fall. The city looked clean and new and somehow washed in the sunlight. Rush found it difficult to believe that the washed look was even less than skin deep. He had the feeling that the bright light ought to cut through the veneer. It was at best a cosmetic cleanliness and the lines should show through under strong light. He turned in at the bank and walked to a teller's window.

"My name is Rush Henry. I believe an account has been opened in my name here."

The teller looked at him appraisingly through the bars of his cage. He seemed satisfied with what he saw.

"Will you step across the lobby to Mr. Brandt at the desk inside the rail? Identify yourself and give him an authorized signature."

That took a few minutes then Rush signed the authorized signature to a check for a thousand dollars. He took it in nine hundreds, four twenties and a pair of tens. The sun was still bright as he came back onto the street and turned toward the offices of the Forest City *Chronicle*. There he asked for Bill Prime. This time Mr. Prime was in and after a brief exchange over an interoffice speaker, Rush was shown into a corner office. A man with a shock of white hair over a ruddy, rugged face was working behind a desk. He looked up as Rush entered and nodded him to a chair.

"Be a minute," he said.

His head ducked down to the paper before him again. With a heavy editorial pencil he marked a piece of copy with solid strokes, scribbled a note on the margin and pushed a buzzer. A girl popped into the office, took the piece of copy and left. Prime looked up at Rush. Without rising he stuck a hand across the table. Rush came over and shook it briefly.

"Mr. Henry?" said Prime.

"Yes," said Rush.

"What can I do for you?"

"Quite a little, I hope," said Rush. "I'm doing a series of articles on industrial cities of the size of Forest City. Trying to show what they're doing in the way of reconversion with a picture of sorts of how the changeover period hits the general public, the merchants, and the factory workers themselves."

"Free lance or assignment?" asked Prime.

"I'm doing them for the Chicago *Express*," said Rush. "I used to work for Pappy Daley and when this came up I was at a loose end and he sent me."

"I asked because if the articles were in our line, I'd like a chance at them. An outsider's views might be news for the *Chronicle*."

"I suspect that Daley would be willing to release them after he's used them," said Rush. "I'll ask him."

"Okay, now what can I do for you?"

"Well, I'd like to borrow a man now and then to steer me a little. I'll figure my own slant but I'll miss a lot of angles if I just push around alone. I'd like a little help from the political angle. That is about city government and its relation to industry and the merchants themselves."

Prime spent a deliberate minute lighting a cigar.

"We have a rather unusual political set up in Forest City. It might be wise to leave it alone. Or at least cover it from a distance."

Rush raised a polite eyebrow.

Prime looked at the end of his cigar, then, satisfied with his light, he looked back at Rush.

"Your name is familiar. Haven't I heard of you somewhere before?"

"Possibly," said Rush noncommitally.

"You know, of course, that I can get a rewrite on your history in something less than an hour from our Chicago correspondent."

Rush looked up to find Prime grinning at him. He grinned back.

"Yes," he said, "I know that. As a matter of fact

I would rather have let that slide so that my history wouldn't influence you either way in giving me the help I want." He leaned back in his chair and looked at the ceiling for a moment. "Your Chicago correspondent would tell you that I haven't worked for the *Express* for better than five years. Outside of the time I spent in the army, he'd tell you that I have been a private detective with my own agency in Chicago. I am, however, a reporter too. My guild card is still up to date and I can go to work in Chicago tomorrow if I want to."

Prime smiled a little.

"I remember now. There was something about some emeralds. Old Germaine's kids got in trouble over them some way and you cleaned it up. I cubbed in Chicago a long time ago, and I've still got some good contacts there. So now you're writing articles on industrial cities." His smile was now one of polite disbelief.

"Yes," said Rush ignoring the smile.

"You wouldn't have a side angle on local politics? You mentioned that."

"That's always pertinent," said Rush.

"You'll never find it as pertinent as it is here. I wonder if you know what you're getting into."

"Maybe you could tell me," said Rush.

"I could, indeed. But I won't. I'll let you dig around. Oh, I'll give you some help but you're on your own." His cigar was dead and he put another match to it. He puffed thoughtfully for a moment as if deciding how much to say. Then he leaned forward across the desk.

"You look as though you could take care of yourself but let me make a point. I've run a newspaper in this town for over twenty years. I know it as well as any man can under those circumstances. It's a stinking hellhole of a city. You remember Chicago in the twenties. That's Forest City in the forties, in the thirties, too. The boys here are smarter. They make it look good. Nobody can put their finger on a thing so the voters keep sending the same people back every year. It's damn near a dictatorship. It's a vicious, violent, sinful city and if I were raising a family I'd move. I'm a bachelor and I'm odd enough to sit around and see what happens. Something will sometime and I want to be there. It'll be great news. In the meantime I'm just sitting here watching, keeping my nose clean, and keeping quiet. I don't want a bomb in my plant or an 'accident' in my car. I want to be around for the pay-off. Now, if these articles of yours just happen to be aimed at an expose of Forest City, that's fine. I'll sit back and watch. Anything I can do without being caught I'll do, but you're on your own." He grinned at Rush and put a third match to the stump of his cigar.

"Of course, if it looks like you were getting anywhere I might help a little more. I've got an intense feeling of civic pride but it's not half as intense as my love of my own hide. I'm too old not to have odds when I start to fight."

Rush smiled at him. It was a smile that admitted nothing.

"That's very interesting, Mr. Prime. Sidelights like that are what make an article interesting. However, expose is a pretty big term. If anything turns up I'll put it in the articles."

"You're not putting out a thing, are you?"

"No," said Rush. "Not a thing."

"Okay, I've got just the man to help you. He knows this town inside out."

He lifted a phone and spoke briefly.

"Ask Matt Pedrick if he'll come in," he said. He cradled the phone and looked back at Rush. "Matt's one of our columnists. He hasn't got a regular beat, he just covers what he likes, gossip mostly. Actually he's working for laughs. I pay him a lot of dough but he doesn't need it. He came in here five or six years ago and offered to do a column for free. I paid him a little something to have some kind of control over him. It was good. It sold a lot of papers so I've paid him more for it through the years. He's dug up contacts and sources that nobody else in town can touch. He's a nice guy, too. You'll like him. I have an idea you talk the same language."

The office door opened and a man stepped out of

the pages of *Esquire* and into the room. So there *is* someone on whom those clothes look good, thought Rush. Besides Bing Crosby, he added. His eye made its habitual photograph of the man. Five ten to eleven, medium brown hair, gray eyes, smooth skin stretched nicely over cheekbones that just missed being high. One eyebrow grew into what might be a permanent lift. The shoulders were not broad but there was enough narrowness at the hips to give an impression of strength and physical condition. A deep tan completed an impression of health. The man walked over and stood beside the desk.

"Matt, this is Rush Henry. Henry, Matt Pedrick," said Prime.

They shook hands and Pedrick's grip was solid.

"Henry's doing a series of articles on Forest City for the Chicago *Express*, Matt. He wants some background—social and political and I told him you were the man for the job."

Pedrick's eyebrow lifted higher at the word 'political.' He repeated it. "Political?"

Prime nodded.

"Yes. Naive, isn't he? About Forest City, that is."

"That's quite an assignment, Bill," said Matt Pedrick. "Who's going to write my column for the next week or so while I tell him?"

Rush got into the conversation.

"I'm afraid you're over-estimating what I want.

I mainly want someone to come to with questions I can't get answered anywhere else. There are a lot of things I want to know that I could probably dig out alone, but someone on the ground floor could tell me in a matter of minutes what it might take me days to get by myself."

Pedrick grinned at him.

"I was kidding, Henry. I'll do anything I can for you." Prime shuffled some papers on his desk. "Come on down to my office. Bill has to make like he's working. We can talk there."

He led the way down a hall lined with glazed glass doors to a corner office. He opened the door and motioned Rush ahead of him. Rush took two steps into the room and stopped. Pedrick came to stand at his shoulder. Rush looked for a pair of minutes, his eyes wandering over the room. If Pedrick's clothes were Hollywood, his office was strictly Cecil B. DeMille. He looked around for an onyx bathtub. He let his head turn slowly till his eyes met Pedrick's. They were narrowed in a pleased smile.

"Gaudy, isn't it?" he said.

Footsteps tapped lightly down the hall behind them and a girl walked past them and sat at the second desk in the room. She completed the picture. Pure MGM.

"Kit, this is Rush Henry," said Pedrick. "My girl Friday, Henry. Kit English."

Rush took a deep breath.

"Things have changed," he said in a dazed voice. "The newspaper business was never like this when I was a leg man."

Pedrick laughed.

"You like it?"

"I wonder if Mr. Prime needs another columnist. When I worked for the *Express* they hired their female help on the principle that you should keep your eyes on your work not on the female help." Kit English looked up from her desk and smiled a cool smile. "And interior decoration was something done by a bootlegger."

"Don't blame Bill for this layout or for Kit," said Pedrick. "I did it myself. Kit works for me, not the *Chronicle*. I didn't want money for my column, but since Bill insisted on paying I stuck it into decorating this room and paying Kit. It's gaudy all right, but impressive. A lot of people come up here to tell me things and a lot of them are impressed. They walk in here and they get the idea that they're talking to Winchell. It helps a lot."

"I can see how it would," said Rush. "I'm fighting the temptation to tell you my life story myself."

"I'd be charmed. Do you want Kit to take notes?"

"No," said Rush. "I'll save that till I know you

better, you and Miss English. Tell me," he said, "isn't that a bar in the corner. I go to a movie now and then and that square thing in the corner always turns out to be a bar in offices like this."

"No," said Pedrick, "that's just a file cabinet. This is the bar."

He walked to photographic mural of Forest City on one wall and touched the metal name plate at its base. It swung back from the wall. The back of the picture was lined with racks for glasses and the opening it had covered held a shelf of bottles and a midget refrigerating unit for ice cubes.

"What will you have?" asked Pedrick.

Rush walked to the opening and peered at the bottles.

"That," he said, pointing at a bottle of Old Overholt rye.

"Water, seltzer or soda?" asked Pedrick.

"Just that and a glass," said Rush.

He poured four fingers in a highball glass and watched as Pedrick squirted seltzer on Scotch in two glasses, one of which he handed to Kit. The girl turned away from her desk to join them and crossed her legs. Rush got the impression that it was a studied gesture. It was an easy impression to get from a pair of legs as displayable as hers. Then he looked at her face and realized that it was not studied at all. Her attention was fully on him. Her appraisal was expert. Rush didn't know how he knew but he was certain that she had him tabbed as surely as an expert would appraise a rough diamond. He felt a little rough under her scrutiny. The concentration and the intelligence it implied were a little startling in such a lovely face framed by such lovely blonde hair.

"Now, let's get to your problems," said Pedrick. "You want to know about Forest City. Bill said something about politics."

"He put words in my mouth. The insistence on politics is strictly his. But every time the word is mentioned in connection with Forest City everybody looks around the room as if the walls had ears and almost whispers. Maybe I should hear about politics. What is there about them that inspires such respect?"

"I don't think respect is quite the words," said Pedrick. "In the normal sense of the word, there is no such thing as politics in Forest City. That is, we have no political parties. Oh, there's usually a reform ticket in elections. I believe there is one with a slate for the elections due in the next week or so. But they never have a chance. The incumbents never lose. They've been in so long they've grown roots. They'll be there for another twenty years, or until they die. Then they'll have someone just like them to move in and graft on to the same roots. It's perpetual motion, only there's never any motion. They just sit, collect and get re-elected."

"You wouldn't want to put a name to several of those 'theys'," said Rush.

"Which ones?" asked Pedrick.

"These incumbents you mentioned and the 'they' you suggest are behind them. They interest me."

"I can do better than name them. I can introduce them to you. I'm having a kind of party at my apartment tonight and quite a few of them will be there. How about you, can you come?"

"I certainly can," said Rush, "and thanks a lot."

"Think nothing of it." He looked at Kit. "Maybe we can fix him up with a lady. Nothing's too good for a visiting newspaperman."

Kit looked thoughtfully at Rush.

"I don't think I'd have any trouble," she said. "Let me make a few calls."

Rush remembered the girl named Gay Wimberly.

"Don't bother," he said. "That is, if it's all right if I bring my own guest."

Pedrick looked at him in surprise.

"When did you get in town?" he asked.

"Yesterday afternoon," Rush said. "Why?"

"That's fast work, son."

Kit looked at him and Rush could see her appraisal undergoing a slight revision. Upward or downward, he couldn't tell.

"You should see me in Chicago," he said and leered directly at Kit. Stick that in your appraisal and add it up, he thought.

Chapter 5

Rush learned via Mr. Bell's admirable invention that Miss Wimberly would be both charmed and available, but not until some time after ten o'clock. The Blue Goose, that being the name of the establishment that required her presence, could dispense with her after that time. Rush promised to call for her and spent the rest of the day nosing around, getting the feel of Forest City. He placed bets on horses at a pair of places with no success. In passing he noted that the horse parlors did a hell of a business. Men in shirt sleeves darted in to place a pair of dollars and whisked out immediately after the race was called. There seemed to be quite a bit of business transacted by phone. In both places a battery of telephones were manned by men in eyeshades and gartered shirt sleeves. They handled telephone, cigarette and pencil with practiced ease, making notations on scratch pads on the desk before them and tearing them off to hand to runners who took them to the central book. It was all very efficient in a practiced way. The grooves they ran in were well worn through long use.

The way of life common to Forest City began to come up through the veneer. They had had gambling for so long that is seemed as usual as a Sunday game of golf. Familiarity had bred complaisance. They were for the most part, however, a very unsophisticated set of gamblers—these men who laid their money against the house. Rush kept track of the odds paid on half a dozen races, making a note on the back of a scratch sheet. There was something wrong somewhere. He also noted odds quoted on all the horses in several races. It didn't figure. The bookies were running something close to a hundred and twenty-five percent book. Seldom did a horse draw as much as 20-1 odds and often two horses in a race were at even money. The odds were shaved all down the line to a point where the house was a lead-pipe cinch in every race. It could only happen in a closed corporation. There had to be cooperation between all bookmakers or competition would give the bettors a better break. If everybody stuck together they could put odds where they wanted them and to hell with the betting public. They only had to be careful to give long enough odds on an outsider or two to tempt long money bettors. The odds on the favorites were short enough to cover almost any combination of winners.

Rush stopped in his room for a drink before dinner and placed a call to the *Express* in Chicago. He asked for the sports editor.

"Tommy, this is Rush Henry," he said when his call came through.

"What's on your mind, Speedy?" asked the editor.

"I want some track odds on some races run this afternoon. Give me the mutuel payoff on them." He named a half dozen races. Tommy had them for him in a matter of sixty seconds.

"Thanks, Tommy. Buy yourself a drink and I'll pay for it when I get back."

He hung up and compared figures. He had been right. In almost every case the mutuel odds paid were higher by as much as eight dollars than those paid in Forest City. It was a nice racket. A new one, too. It was the same as shooting craps with loaded dice, or playing poker with marked cards. The only weakness was that you had to have a spot like Forest City to work it.

He showered, shaved, changed clothes and ate in the hotel coffee shop. At eight-thirty he caught a cab to the address Pedrick had given him. Kit English met him at the door. She wore a hostess gown of black velvet that made her blonde hair gleam like the flame on a candle. She seemed very much at home, almost as though she lived here. Rush figured the odds that she did in practice if not in fact were about twenty to one, even by Forest City standards.

"Come in, Mr. Henry," she said. Then she peered over his shoulder. "I thought you were bringing a guest," she added.

"I am," said Rush. "She won't be available till after ten o'clock, however. I'll go get her then."

Pedrick came up then to stand with his arm around her shoulders.

"Where's your young lady, Henry?" he asked. "I hope you're not going to spoil the picture I had built up of you. A Casanova from Chicago." There was no malice in the words. It was exactly the kind of off-hand, friendly needling that every newspaperman gives every other newspaper man.

"I can spoil that picture in about thirty seconds," said Rush. "Women think of me as a brother. But I do have a girl. She's busy till ten. I'll pick her up then."

"One of your sisters, no doubt," said Kit English, and there was malice in these words.

"Very sisterly," said Rush.

"How are you going to get her?" asked Pedrick.

"I'll call a cab."

"Take my car," said Pedrick. "You'll get a cab at ten o'clock at night some Tuesday in June." He tossed a leather folder of keys to Rush. "It's the Buick convertible at the curb."

"Thanks a lot," said Rush. "I'll be very impressive in a Buick convertible."

"Yes," said Kit English, "maybe she'll think of you as only a half brother."

"Put your tongue back in its sheath, dear," said Pedrick. "Come on, Henry, meet some of my guests."

In the next fifteen minutes Rush met people at

the rate of a new name every thirty seconds. Only three of them were familiar. Mayor Patrick Gunn, Police Commissioner Mark Carver, and Max Carney. Rush searched his mental files on Carney. He came up with the two words, Liquor and Rackets.

This rather mild looking Irishman might have just walked off a construction job. His voice had the hoarseness associated with bellowing orders over the noise of riveting machines. His face was weathered and his eyes crinkled from facing many a wind and squinting into many a sun. Only his hands gave him away. No hod had calloused those hands within a score of years. The fingers were stubby and perhaps a little gnarled but the skin was smooth and white and the nails had had the undivided attention of an expert manicurist. He was very happy to meet Mr. Henry.

"Articles, eh?" he said. "That's good. Forest City is a nice little place. Clean. We're proud of her. Give us a good story, young man. Let those people in Chicago know that we're up and coming."

Mark Carver had been standing in another conversational circle, but the word 'articles' caught his ear. He did an about face and was part of the group around Carney. He looked at Rush.

"You're writing an article about Forest City, young man?" He asked. Rush nodded.

"I understood you were working for a Chicago

paper. What would they be interested in here?"

Rush patiently explained that it wasn't Forest City alone. That he was doing a series on towns similar to Forest City. By now he had told the story so many times that he had to stop and think to realize that it wasn't true.

"Pat should be interested in this," said Carver. "Pat!" he called across the room. The mayor, a stock character if Rush had ever seen one, came across the room, pausing only to pick up a fresh drink. He had obviously picked up more than one fresh drink in passing. His eyes focused on Carver with a faint effort.

"What's on your mind, Mark?" he asked.

"Henry, here is doing an article on Forest City for a Chicago paper. I think we ought to give him all the cooperation we possibly can."

"Sure," said his Honor. "I'll cooperate. Whaddaya want, young fellow?"

Rush began to resent being called a young fellow. Carver answered the question for him.

"I think it would be a good idea to send a man around with him. He's new in town and one of our boys could show him the ins and outs of the place and save him a lot of time."

And be sure I saw the right things, thought Rush. Aloud he said, "Mr. Pedrick has offered to help me out. I appreciate your offer, though."

Carver looked briefly at Carney and back to

Rush. Rush wondered if he read the glance correctly. To him it said, let's watch this guy. He may dig around and find something. Keep it clean but keep an eye on him. It said all that in a glance that lasted at most a tenth of a second. Aloud to Rush, Carver said:

"That's fine. You couldn't get a better guide than Matt. He knows the town inside out. He helps bury all the skeletons. If you come up against anything we can give you, feel free to ask. Pat or I will have all the figures you can use and maybe we can give you a little more actual history than Matt. We've been around a long time."

Rush got the feeling that the sentence also said, and we'll be here a long time. Pedrick came up then and put a hand on Rush's shoulder.

"Ten o'clock, Henry," he said. "Don't keep your young lady waiting."

Rush thanked him for the reminder and made his excuses. Outside the night air was cool and smooth with the smoothness that only comes in late October. It had a velvet feel as it coursed past his face around the windshield of the open car. He drew up in the No Parking zone in front of the Blue Goose and killed the engine.

Gay Wimberly met him almost at the door. She had a white wrap thrown loosely over bare shoulders. The green gown of the evening before had been replaced with a russet creation. There, to

Rush's masculine eyes, the difference ended. It clung with the same faithfulness to each curve. It was held up, minus straps, by the same miracle. It fell in the same flowing lines to the floor. She walked across the entrance way to meet Rush with grace, yet with a freedom that spoke of long slender legs that had to be lovely. The rest of her was impossible otherwise.

Rush held out an elbow and she rested a hand on it in a regal gesture. He pivoted and led her to the street, feeling very grand. He installed her in the right hand seat of Pedrick's convertible and walked around to get under the wheel. The car was in motion before either of them spoke.

"This," said Gay, "is life. I wonder what the poor people are doing."

"Probably wondering the same thing about the rich."

"Where is it we're going?" she asked.

"Matt Pedrick's apartment. He's partying for quite a mob."

"Yes, there would be a mob. I've been there before. I don't think he invites everybody but everybody hears about it one way or the other and they all come."

"Don't worry about us. We were invited."

"Does Kit English know you're bringing me?"

"She knows I'm bringing somebody. I don't think I mentioned who."

Gay's nose wrinkled in a sly little smile.

"We'll have a lot of fun then. Kit loves me like a sister. A step sister named Cinderella."

"What does she have against you?"

"A date I had with Matt Pedrick once. He is special reserved property and well posted. No trespassing."

"You be very attentive to me," said Rush, "and it'll throw her off the track."

"You're tricky, aren't you?" said Gay. "Do you ever figure out a scheme where you lose?"

"Almost never," said Rush, maneuvering the convertible to the curb. He helped her out of the car and the elevator carried them to Pedrick's apartment. Again the door was opened by Kit English. For a moment, and for the first time, she was almost nonplussed, but only for a moment.

"You have excellent taste, dear," she said looking at a point directly between Rush and Gay. Rush couldn't for the life of him tell to whom she was talking. She turned to Rush. "You weren't gone long, Mr. Henry." That made it a little more obvious. She thought Gay had excellent taste. A compliment from the left hand or southpaw side, as it were. "Come in—we're just about to play a game."

She was wrong. Nobody played any games. The phone rang. Pedrick answered it and handed the receiver to Mark Carver. Carver answered briefly then shouted into the mouthpiece.

"What?"

He listened as someone repeated a message. He turned and cast an undecipherable glance at Mayor Gunn. Then he grunted a pair of words into the phone and hung it up. Slowly he turned to Gunn who had come across the room toward him.

"That was Hacker," he said. "We've got to leave right away and meet him."

"To hell with him," said Gunn. "I'm just beginning to have fun." His eyes flickered back to the brunette who had had his full attention till now.

"You'll come all right. This is important."

"What's important enough to drag me outa here now when I don't wanta go?" The Mayor's tongue was a touch thick.

Carver looked around the room then shrugged his shoulders.

"Okay—I'll tell you. Somebody just killed Beau Marr. They shot him through a window at his home."

Gunn's jaw dropped, lifted, and worked slowly as though the news was something he must chew thoroughly before digesting. Carney came across the room in two steps.

"Marr shot?" he asked briefly.

Carver nodded.

"Who did it?"

"They don't know," said Carver.

Carney bit off an upper case oath and made a motion with his mouth as though he wanted to spit on the floor.

"Women," he said. "I knew those damn women would get him in trouble some time." He turned to Gunn and Carver. "Well, what're we waiting for? Let's go."

They left in what was almost a rout, walking on each other's heels in their hurry. Rush steered Gay to the bar where Pedrick was standing, elbow on bar, glass in hand, surveying the scene with something resembling amusement.

"What was that?" asked Rush.

"Hello, Gay," said Pedrick. "How did this Rush street Romeo hook you?"

"It was easy. I dropped my handkerchief. He never had a chance."

"That," said Pedrick, turning back to Rush, "was a bombshell such as you never saw lit under two more surprised men. I'll make it three. Tom Hacker, our worthy Chief of Police, is probably giving birth to his third set of broken dishes by now. We haven't had a murder for three years. And it had to be Beau Marr. That's no joke, son."

"Could we just possibly go peek over their shoulders and look through their magnifying glasses?" asked Rush.

"We could but it's not necessary. There's a guy at headquarters that'll give me everything they get in the morning. Come around. We'll look him up together." He looked speculatively at Rush. "That is if you're really interested."

"Oh, I am," said Rush. "The smell of fresh blood brings out the hound in me every time. Tell me something," he added, "what did Max Carney mean when he said the women got him? Did your Mr. Marr have a fast way with females?"

"Yes and no," said Pedrick. "He made many a fast dollar out of them. But he dealt in them as a commodity. I was under the impression that his personal tastes lay in another direction. I might be wrong, even though everybody else thought the same thing."

Rush looked around at the room behind him and turned back to Pedrick with surprise. Pedrick smiled.

"Empty, isn't it. Everybody had the same idea at the same time. Get out of here and go where somebody might know something. That bombshell burned more heels than those worn by the Messrs. Hacker, Carney and Carver."

"Why, that's an act straight out of Mickey Mouse. One minute the room's full, the next it's empty." He put a hand on Gay's arm. "Remind me to hang on to you. Disappearing is too easy here."

"Have a drink and forget it," said Pedrick. He reached over the bar and lifted a bottle and glass to the bar surface. "Pour your own," he directed.

Rush poured three fat fingers and looked at Gay.

"Go right ahead," she said. "Get drunk. And may I join you."

He poured her a pony and they touched rims.

"Happy days," said Rush.

"Merry Christmas," said Gay.

"Many happy returns," said Pedrick who had filled a third glass.

As they set down empty glasses Kit English came back into the room. Without a word she reached for the bottle and poured a straight drink in a glass.

"As long as the party's over I might as well relax," she said.

"Kit takes these affairs very seriously," said Pedrick. "She feels that I should stay sober and entertain my sources. Since I refuse to, she does."

"Somebody has to. Some of your alleged sources would walk away with your furniture if somebody wasn't watching them."

"Lovely people," said Pedrick. "Everyone of them." He looked at Rush, at Gay and at Kit, in that order. "Well, children—what do we do? Since we've whipped our jaded reflexes up to a party we ought to have one."

"Goody," said Gay. "I love parties."

"What would you suggest?" asked Rush. "I'm a stranger here."

"A stranger at the feast, only there isn't any

feast." Pedrick looked at his watch. "We can just catch the show at Carlo's."

They caught the show at Carlo's—the first five minutes of it. Then a shadowy figure slipped into a chair beside Pedrick at the table and whispered into his ear. Pedrick leaned toward Rush and spoke under his breath.

"I'm getting my lowdown a little early. Want to catch this?"

Rush shifted his chair to face away from the floor and toward Pedrick. The girls looked over their shoulders briefly and turned back to the floor.

"This is Little Pete Maxon, Rush. He tells me things now and then. It's okay, Petey," he said at the little one's look of suspicion. "He's okay. What's up?"

"Yuh know Marr got it?" Petey's voice was husky and his whisper seemed habitual as though most of his vocal communication was done sub rosa. Pedrick nodded. "It was through his window. A thirty-eight. They's some footprints, all men's. He leaves no traces."

"Any suspects?"

"Naw. That Hacker couldn't find his nose in a bright light."

"What do the boys downtown think?"

"They got no ideas. Mostly they figure it was some babe's old man or brother or something."

"What's Hacker doing?"

"He's put out a call to pick up all suspicious characters. Hah!"

"Hah, is right. He'll have half the town in the jug."

"They got the time on the nose."

"How?"

"Murphy, Marr's butler hears the shot and is winding his alarm clock at the same time. It is exactly ten-oh-one."

"I'll remember that when I fix up my alibi."

"Hah." Mr. Maxon was amused.

"How much work was it to get to the window?" asked Rush.

"A cinch," said Little Pete. "No wall and bushes for cover all the way. You could hide an army on the front lawn."

"Anything else we ought to know?" asked Pedrick.

"Naw. Police Chief Hacker is very upset at losing such at outstanding citizen in such a manner and will issue a further statement in the morning. Every effort is being made to trace the basta—uh, dastardly criminal. Progress is bein' made and an arrest is expected in a matter of hours." Petey said the words as if by rote. "He says that every time. I know it by heart," he added.

Pedrick dropped something into Petey's palm which lay open on the table.

"Thanks, Little Pete. Keep in touch with things.

If anything breaks, which I don't think it will, let me know."

"Sure. Thanks, boss." He slipped out of his chair and was gone as the lights came up signaling the end of the floor show. The girls turned back to the table and finished drinks at their elbows. It had been, it seemed, a good show. They told Pedrick and Rush what they had missed. They also had one last drink for the road.

In the car driving home there was little talk. Rush's mind seethed with conjecture. The gunning of Beau Marr had not been listed on his agenda. It was an edge, a fingerhold, if he could figure out how to use it. He was still figuring when Pedrick stopped the car before a large apartment house. Gay dug a finger in his ribs.

"You can wake up now. I always insist on being taken to the door."

"Which door?" asked Rush.

"We'll make it the front door. You can come in when you bring your merit badges and a letter from your scoutmaster."

"I'll have them tomorrow. What should my scoutmaster say?"

"All I want is a guarantee that you can start a fire with two matches and tie a square knot." They were at the door now. Gay turned in the dim light from the entrance way and looked at Rush. Her eyes were wide and looked straight into his. Her eyebrows were raised just the faintest fraction of an inch and her mouth looked very soft. "You're a very nice boy," she said. "I hope you manage to stay out of trouble. I don't suppose you will but I wish you would. Now I think you'd better kiss me good night."

She moved a step forward and looked up at Rush. To hell with questions, thought Rush. I'll find out later why she thinks I'll get in trouble. He kissed her. It was a strange kiss. There was certain passion, but the predominant emotion was contentment, a luxurious, peaceful contentment. Gay's were the softest lips in his memory and they moved faintly under his. Time seemed to fall away and he was surprised and a little embarrassed when she moved away.

"That will have to do for now," she said.

"Thank you," said Rush knowing she would know for what he was thanking her. He turned and walked down the flagstone path to the street and was surprised that his breath came faster than before.

Chapter 6

Pedrick let Rush out at his hotel and he walked through the lobby to the tap room. There he took a stool at the bar and ordered a double rye. He drank it in slow silence. Looking at but not seeing his own reflection in the mirror. The murder of Marr had no place in his picture. They didn't murder people in Forest City. It was too well organized. He scouted briefly the idea that a suddenly outraged father of one of Marr's ladies for hire had decided to avenge his daughter's honor, and discarded it. It was Rush's experience that if the ladies had fathers, they were probably being kept in booze by their daughters. Somebody wanted Marr out of the way and that fact in itself pointed to a rift in the lute. All was not well among the men who ran Forest City.

It also pointed a path for Rush. Nothing boils a pot like suspicion. It seemed that suspicion was indicated and it was obviously up to Rush to supply it. An idea sprang full blown into his brain and he grinned at his face in the mirror. He felt a little like Red Skelton's mean little boy. He tapped his glass on the bar for the bartender.

"Another double," he said.

The bartender looked at him, then shrugged and

poured the drink. He turned back to the cash register to ring up the sale. Rush poured the rye in the spittoon at his feet. When the bartender turned around his glass was empty. He pointed at it.

"Another?" asked the bartender. His voice was flat but his eyebrows said 'I'm gonna have trouble with this guy before the night is out.'

He did. Rush ordered double ryes as fast as he could pour them out without being seen. He became noisy. He became semi-insulting when the bartender was slow. He finally half fell off his stool. When he ordered another double rye after that the bartender looked at him in some disgust. He pointed a finger past Rush's shoulder at the door.

"Out," he said.

Out he meant. Rush put up a maudlin battle for another drink but it was a losing one. The bartender had only one word left for Rush. 'Out.'

With hurt dignity Rush pushed himself off the stool, steadied himself against a table and stalked in a roundhouse curve out of the bar. In the lobby he managed to collide with a potted palm, a bellhop and a divan. He became entangled in the leash of a dog led by an elderly female. He mumbled under his breath and finally allowed the bellhop to point him at the elevators after having gotten his key for him. The elevator operator wakened him at his floor and led him down the hall to his room where he opened the door and helped Rush to the bed.

Rush relaxed on the bed and mumbled that he was all right. The operator took off his shoes and quietly left the room. Rush waited till he heard the clang of the elevator door then tiptoed to his own door and locked it. He went to the bottle on his dresser and poured a drink. He downed it and looked owlishly at his reflection in the mirror. It had been a good job, he thought, good enough at least. Some five or six people would testify that he was stinking drunk at one o'clock. The elevator boy would remember having poured him into bed. His alibi was prepared in advance. He set a small alarm clock for three o'clock and lay down to sleep.

He was dreaming of cascading red hair flowing over his face in flaming waves when the alarm sounded. He silenced it with a stab of his hand and flipped on the light. He took a short drink from the neck of the bottle and put his shoes back on. At the bed table he flipped the pages of the directory and made a brief mental note.

Then Rush dug a flashlight out of his suitcase and slipped it into a side pocket. A small leather covered blackjack went into his hip pocket and a small steel jimmy hung over his belt with the long part inside his pants at the hip. He checked his equipment briefly and went to the door. He listened with his ear to the thin paneling for a minute then slipped out locking the door behind him.

Instead of turning for the elevator he headed for the rear of the hotel. There, as he had expected, he found a service elevator and service stairs. He used the stairs to descend the seven floors to the ground level. It was an uninterrupted trip. He found a door open and stepped out into an alley. His footsteps were loud in the silence as he walked to the mouth of the alley and peered into the open street. It was deserted. A small bar across the street was lit by a single light and a man behind a cash register was counting money. Rush turned left, away from the main street and walked a half block. Then he turned right again and walked steadily for almost a mile. He stopped for a moment, checked his mental note against a street address and turned right for a block, stopping at the corner and looking to his left down the street. The sign he expected to see hung there against the dull late night sky. It was unlit now, but an hour earlier it had glowed its neon brightness in the letters *Sully's*.

Rush retraced his steps a half block to the alley and turned right. A few more steps brought him to an areaway and a door marked with a sign. It said 'employees entrance.' His jimmy was out of his belt and almost to the door when footsteps sounded somewhere behind him. Instantly he faded into the recessed shadow of the door and brought his blackjack from his hip pocket. A figure turned the corner into the areaway and walked to the door. With some regret Rush took a step forward and laid his blackjack expertly alongside the temple of the man who came toward him. He caught him as he slumped. With probing fingers he felt the spot he had slugged. It was a neat job. The man would sleep quite peacefully for an hour or two and waken with nothing but a bad headache and probably a lost job. Rush searched farther with his fingers and felt better about slugging the man. In a shoulder holster was an ugly short nosed .38, a belly gun. He was, in fact, glad he had slugged first and felt afterwards. He was not armed for an argument with a .38. He pulled the man into the shadow of the building and returned to his task of opening the door.

In a matter of seconds he split wood from wood and the door sprung open. He stepped inside and his nose told him he was in a kitchen. Shading his flashlight with his fingers to leave a thin wedge of light he stepped past ovens and tables toward a pair of double swinging doors. On the other side of them was his destination, Mr. Card Sully's pride and joy, a thing of beauty indeed. As neat a night club as Rush had ever visited in the dead of night. He looked around him at the gleaming tables, at the back bar with its pyramided glass sparkling in the dim light of his flash. From the ceiling swung a mamoth glass chandelier, a magnificent object. Rush looked at it and decided to save it for last. With a sigh of pure joy he moved behind the bar and found a bottle of Old Overholt. He lifted the bottle to his lips and drank deeply. Then he swung around to look at the back bar. He kissed the bottle lightly and heaved it with all his might at a towering stack of glasses. They rained to the floor in a thousand pieces and a tremendous star appeared in the large mirror behind them.

Again the sigh of almost boyish glee and then Rush went to work seriously. He smashed every glass and every mirror behind the bar. The whiskey bottles he heaved at the chandelier, chipping away at its garish magnificence. With his jimmy he loosened the bar itself from the floor and turned it over on its side. From the kitchen he brought a can of lye well mixed with hot water. This he sloshed over the midget dance floor. Chairs and tables he stacked at one side of the room, and poured more of the lye over the rich carpeting. Drapes came tumbling down to be sprinkled with a rich mixture of bourbon, scotch and gin. He opened bottles of champagne and fizzed them at the oil paintings with which Sully had decorated the few bare walls. Then at last he turned to the chandelier, now not so beautiful. Standing on a chair on a table he pried it loose from its moorings with his invaluable jimmy and watched with deep satisfaction as it crashed

to the floor. Then he stepped back into the doorway and threw the full beam of his flashlight over
the room. A flock of locusts with the aid of Lil'
Abner's turnip termites couldn't have done a better job. It was a complete, a total and final
wreck.

Let Mr. Sully figure out who did that, thought
Rush. That should prove enough suspicion to last
for at least twenty-four hours. Then he could stir
up another batch. Coupled with Beau Marr's murder it should start the ruling gentry of Forest City
to wearing armored vests and carrying knives. It
seemed a shame, but the only way to upset the
nice, even comfortable flow of very commercial vice
in this pretty city was to blast a little open hell
at it.

With the consciousness of a job well done Rush
left Sully's and a half hour later was in his room
in the hotel. To all appearances he might never have
left it. He carefully stowed his jimmy in the reser-
voir of his toilet and hung the blackjack on a nail
outside his window. Then he peacefully undressed
and as peacefully slept until nine o'clock.

He might have slept longer but a dream finally
got too much for him. He was under Niagara
Falls with his mouth open trying to swallow all the
water coming at him. He awakened to find a small
wiry man with tight curly hair calmly pouring a
glass of water into his open mouth.

"Robin Twist, you son of an ancient dog!" he shouted.

"Hi, Rush," said Robin.

"Put that water down you Scotch termite. Are you trying to drown me?"

"Why, no, Boss. I'm just improving employee-employer relations."

Rush sat up on the edge of the bed and looked at him.

"That's right, you are working for me now. Well, let's have a little more respect."

"Hah," said Robin succinctly.

Rush grinned at him through a yawn.

"I'm glad to see you, you blasted midget. I think I'm going to need you bad."

While Rush shaved, showered and dressed he gave Robin a fill-in on what had gone before, ending with a once over on his raid of the previous evening. Robin was unhappy.

"You get all the fun. Why couldn't you wait till tonight? All my life I've wanted to wreck a bar and the bouncers were always too big. Now you wreck one with not a bouncer in sight. It should happen to a pig."

"You'll get plenty of wrecking of your own to do. Maybe when you grow up, I'll give you a bar of your own and you can go all out."

Robin's oath was unseemly on the lips of such a harmless looking little man.

"When did you leave Uncle Sam?" asked Rush.

"A week ago. We parted the best of friends."

"Did you see the Colonel?"

"I had lunch with him the day I shed my military bearing. He sent his best to you." Robin lit a cigarette. "A great guy," he said.

"Yes," said Rush. That took care of the Colonel, their late superior in G-2. The Colonel himself couldn't have asked for a better farewell.

"What do you want me to do?" asked Robin.

"You, my miniature Dr. Gallup, are going to feel the pulse of the nation, or at least of Forest City. You are going to influence people and form public opinion."

"A task for which I am eminently fitted. I'll find me a blonde pulse and feel it all afternoon. There'll be no charge for this service."

"You will stay away from blondes. You will seek the company of middle aged business men, at a bar perferably when they have relaxed. Find out what they think about Marr's death and about the wrecking of Sully's joint when it gets out. Intimate that you have inside information that gang warfare has come to Forest City. Say you have heard that Max Carney imported gorillas from Chicago to do the work. Be a little dark cloud on the horizon. Go about spreading gloom about the fair name of Forest City and how it is about to be dragged through the mud of a nasty gang war."

"Should I do all that this afternoon or should I save some of it for tomorrow?" asked Robin.

"I estimate that you should spend at least three days at it. In the meantime keep away from me. Here," he threw a wad of money on the bed. "Take this and get a room at another hotel. Let me see." He picked up the directory and looked up Hotels. "Register at the Plains Hotel. Use your own name. Write me a letter every day and send it care of General Delivery. Only phone in case of emergency. And for Pete's sake keep out of trouble. Pick your spots. Don't try and tell Max Carney himself that he's importing torpedoes. Watch it as never before."

"Can do," said Robin. "And in this same meantime you'll be doing what? Squiring blondes?"

"I'm glad you reminded me. I'm taking a ravishing blonde to the dog races this afternoon. This is Sunday, isn't it?"

"It is and you are a name of a name of a name. I think I'll follow you in the streets and beg you to come home to mother."

"If you do I'll call you by the name you so richly deserve. I'll also take you across my knee and spank you. Now, get going. I'll meet you in this room Tuesday night at one o'clock. Get in the same way you did this morning with your trusty little pick lock."

Robin grinned.

"They sure taught us some neat little tricks in the war, didn't they, papa?"

"They did and the neatest of them was this."

Rush picked Robin up under one arm and opened the door with the other. He deposited the little man in the hallway outside.

"On your way, pixie," he said and shut the door in Robin's face.

Rush finished dressing with care. Robin's chance remark about blondes reminded him that he had contracted to escort Kit English to the dog races. Pedrick and Gay were both engaged, not with each other Rush hoped, and the two spares made it a date.

He ate in the coffee shop and called a cab which deposited him on Kit English's doorstep at two o'clock sharp. The doorstep belonged to a small cottage set well back from a quiet street. Kit herself met him at the door. Her hat was on her head and her bag was in her hand. She shut the door behind her and walked down the steps to the street.

"Mother's resting or I would have invited you in," she explained.

Rush looked at her again. He had never imagined her with parents. She was of the highly polished, tough, sharp, new breed of girls that seem to spring into the world full blown.

"We'll take my car," said Kit. "It's around in the garage."

She led the way to the rear of the house and motioned Rush into the driver's seat of the modest coupe sitting in the driveway. They were rolling toward the coliseum before a word broke the silence.

"You're an odd person," said Kit.

"I'm glad you think so," said Rush. "I've made it a point to rise above the herd."

"You'd have done that anyway," she said. "But it's hard to picture you as a writer of articles. You're more the adventurous, man of action type."

Rush wondered what she was getting at. Pedrick must not have told her of his background, or did Pedrick know yet? Maybe Prime hadn't told Pedrick. Maybe Miss English was just digging. He decided it wouldn't hurt to give her something to chew on.

"Well, as a matter of fact, I'm not a full time writer of articles. I'm just doing a favor for an old friend. I used to be a leg man on the Chicago *Express* and when Pappy Daley needed a man for this job he called me. He was a man short and needed help."

"What did he call you from?"

"I run a detective agency in Chicago. I wasn't detecting at the minute and my organization pretty well runs itself so I told Pappy I was available." He stifled a grin at the thought of his 'organization.' Gertrude and Wilmer. Oh yes, and now Robin Twist. He was growing.

"That fits much better. You could be a detective, all right."

Lady, I am a detective, thought Rush. I'm real strong, but I'm smart, too.

They parked in the lot and by-passed a line, at the ticket windows, Kit's press pass taking them into the press box. The first race was ten minutes away and Rush filled the time inspecting the track and the crowd. Kit studied a form chart and marked choices on a scratch sheet. Then she handed Rush her bets and money to cover them. Rush handed the money back.

"I'm on an expense account. It'll stand a little minor betting."

He shouldered his way through the crowd to the bookmaker's windows. It was an odd situation. It was not mutual betting. Bookmakers made bets from behind windows. Their odds were chalked on a slate outside the window. A short inspection told Rush that the same thing happened here as happened in the horse parlors. Odds on for two favorites and short odds for all other entries. Heads I win, tails you lose. He placed Kit's bets with a bet or two for himself on the longest shots he could find.

Back in the box he tried a little pumping of his own.

"Tell me about Pedrick. In all my long and varied newspaper experience, I've never met a columnist like him."

"He's odd, too," said Kit. "He doesn't have to work. His father was a pioneer in Forest City. He made a lot of money in lumber and contracting. Matt went to school at Princeton and stayed on in New York. He was quite a young man about town there for several years. Then his father died and he was the last Pedrick alive so he came back here to live. To keep from dying of boredom he started the column. His name gave him an entry all over town. Outside of that he writes a darn good column. Read it some time. You have to respect the guy. He gets by on ability and hard work when he doesn't need to turn a hand."

It was a long speech and the first race was started before it was through. The rabbit won as usual and Kit's choice was a poor fourth. She tore up her tickets and started to talk but stopped at activity in the box behind them. A short stocky man with graying hair and a permanent twist that was almost a sneer at one corner of his mouth was entering the box. Behind him came a retinue. That was the only way Rush could describe it. First the armed guard, their arms bulging at their shoulders. They spread and sat, one in each corner of the box. Then the palace favorites. They surrounded the short man and helped him to his seat and saw to his comfort.

Then the hangers on. They filled the box and tried to get a word in edgewise to the great man.

Rush looked him over carefuly and turned back to Kit.

"That would be our Mr. Sully," he said.

"It would."

"He's heard about Mr. Marr and he's taking no chances." Rush indicated the men in the four corners of the box.

"If you were Mr. Sully, wouldn't you?" she asked.

"If I were Mr. Sully I'd be in my house with the blinds drawn and a squad of tanks on the front lawn. I'd be scared to death."

"A big bold detective like you?" she asked.

"I'd rather be a big old detective if I have my choice."

The second race was being called and they turned their attention back to the track. The rabbit got its head start and the dogs were off. In the semi silence following the initial roar Rush heard further commotion to the rear. He turned and saw a man forcing his way through the hangers on to Sully's side. The King's messenger, he thought. The excited voice of the man penetrated the crowd noise briefly and Rush caught two words. Joint and wrecked. Sully's face turned to stone. He spoke briefly to the men on each side of him. The word was passed and the exodus began. First the hangers on then the favorites and last King Sully with two armed guards fore and two aft. They were gone in a matter of sixty seconds.

"Now, I wonder what that was," said Rush to Kit who was also watching with a puzzled look on her face.

"I don't know, but I'd be a damn poor newspaperman's girl Friday if I didn't try and find out. Come on."

She led the way out of the coliseum. On the street they looked both ways, but they were too late. Sully et al were gone.

"Let's find a phone," she said. "I've got to find Pedrick."

That's for me, thought Rush. I'd like a native son's opinion of things as they are and things as they seem to be in Forest City. He followed her without another word.

Chapter 7

Kit found Pedrick at his apartment. He agreed to meet them at Carlo's in an hour for a drink. He was inclined to minimize the importance of Sully's actions but he had finished his work and felt like company.

Rush drove Kit's car to Carlo's and parked in the lot reserved for customers. It seemed that there were a lot of customers, even on Sunday. He wondered if they gambled on Sunday, too. Kit said they did. Gambling was on a seven-day week and in some places on a twenty-four-hour day. Inside they found a table and ordered drinks. Pedrick slipped into the booth before the drinks had come.

"Well, let's have it," he said. "What happened to Sully?"

Rush described the exodus of the Sully Entourage. He also added the two words he had heard, elaborated only slightly.

"I don't know whose," he said, "but I got the impression that somebody's joint got wrecked."

Pedrick shook his head.

"I doubt it," he said. "It doesn't make sense. Nobody'd have any reason to wreck any joint in this town. It's too well organized." He thought a moment. "Let me use the phone for a minute. Order me a scotch and water."

He slipped out of the booth. Kit's and Rush's drinks came and Rush relayed Pedrick's order. It came back to the booth before Pedrick. The ice in the drink was well on its way to melting before he returned. Rush saw him coming across the room, walking slowly, shaking his head in stubborn disbelief. He sat down and gulped half his drink before he spoke.

"They wrecked it, all right," he said finally.

"Sully's?" asked Kit.

Pedrick nodded his head. "Sully's," he said. "But good, if my contact his it straight." He downed the rest of his drink. "Do you want to go over there?" he asked.

"As a practicing newspaper man, wouldn't it be more interesting to interview the competition?" asked Rush.

"Not a bad idea," said Matt, "especially since he just came into the room." He raised a hand to wave at a figure standing in the doorway. Max Carney came across the room and slipped into the booth beside Pedrick.

"What do you think, Max?" asked Pedrick. He had no need to explain the question.

Carney was silent for a long time.

"Is this for publication, Matt?" he asked.

"Not if you say not."

"Then, I'll be damned if I know. If this were for publication I'd say that it was an act of vandals or attribute it to juvenile delinquency. But it isn't that at all. I just came from there. Whoever did that wanted the place wrecked. He didn't just mess it up a little, he wrecked it so that it'll be three months before they can reopen it, if then. Whoever did it had a reason, and if you can figure the reason I'll give you a piece of this joint. That's what bothers me. The reason. It bothers Sully, too. He doesn't give a damn about the joint, especially. He can afford to shut up and he can afford to redecorate. He'll make it back in another three months. But why? I don't like it. I don't like it at all."

Rush gave himself a mental pat on the back, a hard one. This was exactly what he had wanted. He threw another hammer in the cogs.

"Do you think it has anything to do with the shooting last night?" he asked.

Carney turned to look at him.

"I don't know, Henry. It doesn't seem possible. There's no reason for either of them. Damn it, it worries me." He stabbed his cigarette viciously into the ashtray. Then more calmly, "We're not giving you a very good picture of our usually peaceful city, are we, Henry?"

"You forget I come from Chicago. We've grown used to this kind of thing." He swallowed his drink and looked up at Carney. "If you ask me this looks like somebody was trying to muscle in. It has all the earmarks. One of the boys gets shot. Another boy gets his joint messed up. That's the way it happens in Chicago. It looks very much like a muscle."

Carney looked at him disbelievingly.

"In this town?" he asked. "Look, you're grown up. Let me give you one of the facts of life in Forest City. We're so well organized here that Capone and his torpedoes couldn't muscle in with the help of the fifth air force. Forget it."

"Those are mighty fine trees," said Rush, "but take a look at the forest. You're organized but good. But for how long? How long do you think citizens in a town the size of Forest City are going to sit still if you get noisy. The way I hear it is that they keep the mayor and his chief of police and police commissioner in because they keep the town quiet. No crime, no shootings, no nothing. What'll they do if they find a nice loud gang war in their laps? And did you ever stop to think that somebody might have that idea and be pushing it?" Rush like the idea so well that he filed it. The idea of electing a reform government appealed to him. It would be the easiest way out if he could do it. The idea, however, didn't appeal to Carney.

"That's a lot of hop," he said. "Anybody big enough to swing a deal like that wouldn't be interested in Forest City."

Rush knew that Carney believed that now. But the germs were well planted. Later he'd remember and think about it again. Rush figured it as another good day's work. He could relax now. Carney was through, too.

"I've got an appointment with Gunn and Hacker and Carver in a few minutes. Maybe they've got some ideas. They've been talking to Card and maybe they've picked up something. Call me tomorrow, Matt. Maybe I'll have something for you."

He lifted his bulk out of the booth and left them. Pedrick looked quizzically at Rush.

"You don't care what you say, or to whom, do you?" he said.

Rush raised his eyebrows.

"Did I say something wrong?" he asked.

"No," said Matt. "You didn't say anything wrong. You might even have been right. But didn't you ever learn never to tell people things that they didn't want to hear?"

"Sure, but what do I care what a comparatively small time gambler in a comparatively small town wants to hear?"

Pedrick grinned.

"You're very refreshing, Henry," he said. "And very naive if you peg Carney as a small time gambler. Capone should clear as much in his best year as Max Carney does in a bad year."

They drank up then and Rush drove Kit home in her car. Pedrick followed and picked him up to take him to the hotel. At the door of the hotel

Pedrick opened the door of the car for Rush.

"Look, my fearless friend from the big bad city. Leave me offer you a piece of advice. You're here to write some articles. It says here in fine print. Good for you. But don't let the bloodhound in you lead you up the wrong alley. Carney, Sully and company don't play rough very often but when they do it's very rough, and nobody ever knows about it. You can do that when you own everything and they own everything."

"Thank you," said Rush, "thank you sincerely. I probably won't pay any attention to you, but thanks anyway."

He closed the door behind him and went into the hotel.

Rush bent over to put his key in the lock of his room door but he didn't get it in. The door swung away from his probing key. He straightened and found himself staring across eighteen inches of space into what he could only describe as a mug. The jaws in the mug worked and sounds come out.

"Come in, Mr. Henry," the sounds said in a grotesque imitation of gentility. The nose of the mug aimed in several directions before it reached a bulbous end. The ears were grade A cauliflower, the brows beetled and scarred, the mouth puffy as though recently well pounded. It looked like the mug of a mug who had just lost a box fight. Rush decided it probably was. He wasn't even surprised to see it there. Now that it was there he realized that he had half expected it, or something like it, to be there.

"It's nice of you to ask me in," he said. He stepped around the body attached to the mug and walked into his room. Seated in a chair was a slightly refined counterpart of the mug.

"Shut the door, Junie," said the one in the chair. The door was shut. "You Rush Henry?" the man in the chair asked.

Rush nodded.

"That's me," he said brightly.

"We got a word for you, buddy. You been in town too long. Why don't you leave?"

"But, I like it here," said Rush even more brightly.

"You won't." It was a statement of accepted fact.

"Oh, but I will. Besides I'm not finished with my business here." Rush obstinately refused to understand.

"You won't. And besides you got no business here."

"This is amazing," said Rush. " How did you find that out?"

"I didn't find it out. I'm telling you. You got no business here. I'm also telling you, get out." The man in the chair went all out to make it obvious, also to make it tough. Rush wondered if the corner of his mouth got tired from so much talking.

"I don't think I understand," he said, understanding quite well but wanting it made very plain.

"I'll fix it so you understand, buddy," said the man in the chair. "I'm telling you to get out of town. If you ain't gone in twenty-four hours it'll be just too bad."

"What'll be just too bad?" asked Rush. He had an idea but he wanted to know.

"Maybe we better give you an idea. Take him, Junior."

"Stand right there a minute, Junior," said Rush. The tone of his voice stopped Junior after one step. "Look, you imitation tough guys. I don't want to lose my temper. I don't want to break your hearts by sending you back to your boss all mussed up, so blow. Get out. Scram. The door is right over there."

"Take him, Junior," said the man in the chair.

Junior took one step. Rush sighed. Junior took another step. He reached out a hamlike paw for Rush. Rush caught it by the wrist, twisted, came under it, pulled the elbow to his shoulder and threw his weight forward, hard. Junior came forward in a flying arc. He lit in a bundle in the lap of the man in the chair. The chair collapsed and they made a writhing heap in the middle of the floor. Rush picked up a leg of the chair which splintered off at his feet. With it he prodded Junior.

"Get up, Junior," he said.

Junior showed fight for as long as it took Rush to slug him along side the temple with the chair leg. He rolled him off the man who had been in the chair and issued directions.

"Get some water and wake that ape up. Get him out of here. And when you get back to whoever sent you tell him you're playing with the older boys now."

They were gone in something under five minutes. Rush relaxed in his chair with a glass of rye in his hand. He was tired and hungry. He couldn't decide whether he was more tired or more hungry so he compromised. He had dinner in bed. He was asleep with a clear conscience at nine o'clock.

There was a package from Chicago for him at the desk in the morning and he opened it in his room after breakfast. He leered at its contents for a moment and decided the time was ripe to talk to Bill Prime again. His suspicion campaign could use the facilities of the press. He thought he could convince Prime that the time was come for all good men to take sides. He whistled as he hid the contents of the package and left the hotel for the offices of the Forest City *Chronicle*.

Bill Prime was in and would see him. He found the white haired editor behind his desk. Prime stopped him before he opened his mouth.

"Let an old man do a little guessing," he said.

"Sure," said Rush. "I'll lay a little six to one you're right. Guess ahead."

"I'm not really guessing. I'm deducting." He held up his hand with the fingers spread. He tabbed one finger. "First you get in town. The next day Beau Marr gets shot. The next night Card Sully's joint gets wrecked. Tonight I'll lay *you* six to one Max Carney's spot has an accident."

"I'd have a man there if I were you," said Rush. "The odds are in favor of it. But, you're not accusing me of shooting Beau Marr, are you?"

"No, I don't think you shot Beau. But you might know who did, or why somebody did. My guess, the one I mentioned, is that you are stage managing a blow off in Forest City. I reread the clips on that deal in Weston. I've got a faint idea of how you work. And I'm damned if I'll swallow that goop about a series of articles."

"I'll stick my chin out an inch or two. I don't know who shot Beau Mar. I don't even have a suspicion of why he was shot. Sully's place is another thing. Off the cuff I might hazard a guess about that. As to a blowoff in Forest City, let's let that slide for a while. Maybe yes, maybe no."

"Why let it slide?" asked Prime. "I'd like to know."

"There are a few things I have to know before I say anything about myself or why I'm in Forest

City. Until I find them out I'm writing articles."

"Okay. Maybe I can tell you what you want to know."

"As a matter of fact," said Rush, "you are the only person who can tell me. Assuming the hypothetical blowoff, I'd have to know where you stand before I light the fire. I'm the last guy in the world to minimize the importance of the press."

Prime started to speak but Rush stopped him and went on.

"I not only have to know where you stand but I have to know how far I can count on you going along. With a good militant paper behind me I'd be a long way on the road to a blowoff, assuming that there was a blowoff on my mind."

"Let's put all those bushes away and stop beating around them," said Prime. "What you want to know is will I go along with you and how far." He raised his eyebrows in question at Rush. Rush nodded. "Okay. I'll tell you. When you first walked in here I told you that I was waiting around to see what happened. I could have gone on to say that I was also waiting around for somebody with enough guts to upset the apple cart. Since I didn't say it then I'll say it now. If you'll guarantee to stick it out I'll get behind you. I'll back you to the hilt. I'll be a private in your army. But you have to come through, too. I haven't crawled out on a limb alone in years and I'm too old to form any new habits." He looked quizzically at Rush. "Is that what you wanted?" he asked.

"That," said Rush, "is enough. Consider yourself enlisted."

"There's only one thing," said Prime. "Why are you doing it?"

"It's a funny thing," said Rush. "I'm doing it because somebody is paying me ten thousand dollars."

"Who, for Pete's sake?" cried Prime.

"I haven't the faintest idea. A firm of lawyers, a very respectable firm by the way, approached me in Chicago and offered me the job. That's all I can tell you. There's a little more but it's not pertinent. Yet," he added.

Prime wrinkled his head and stared off into space for a long minute.

"That loses me," he confessed. "I can't figure anybody who'd do that. But as long as they did I'm glad. It should be a nice brawl. I'm glad it came along before I was too old to enjoy it. Now, what do you want me to do?"

"Not much. Mainly a matter of treatment. I want you to approach the things that have happened and are about to happen from a certain angle. I want you to suggest that there may be gang warfare in the offing. Exaggerate things a little. Incite a little friction between factions if possible. I want everybody to be suspicious of everybody else, and I want the common garden variety of citizen to worry about what's happening to this peaceful little city. We might even elect a reform candidate. That'll settle everything." He paused and thought a moment. "One other thing, as I suggested, you might have a man at Carlo's tonight. Your guess wasn't far off."

"Will do. But do you think a reform mayor can do the trick?"

"With a little help he can and I'll give him the help."

"Will he take it?"

"I'll make sure of that before I get him elected. Election's only a week off, I'll talk to the guy this afternoon and make a deal. We'll clean this rat's nest out as slick as a whistle with a little cooperation."

"Oh, happy day," said Prime. "How about Pedrick. Are you going to tell him?"

"He's a pretty sharp guy. I think he's guessed. I'll tell him when the time comes."

"Okay. I'll have a man at Carlo's tonight."

Rush said good-bye then and left the building. Around the corner he stopped in a bar and entered the phone booth. He looked in the directory and dialed the number listed as Sully's. He put a handkerchief over the mouthpiece of the phone and spoke only a few odd sentences to the voice that answered.

"Tell Sully that if he's smart he'll have a couple

of guys at Carlo's tonight. He'll want to know what goes on there."

Rush stilled the voice that sputtered questions into the receiver by replacing it on the hook. Then he walked out of the booth and the bar with a smile of almost childish malice on his face.

Chapter 8

Rush stopped by Gay's apartment at nine. Monday was her day off. She had a drink ready for him while she finished dressing. He was reading the titles of books in a small shelf when she came back into the living room. She had a drink in one hand and a cigarette in the other.

"Can a lady have a light?" she asked.

Rush held a match to her cigarette. She sank back onto the davenport as the tip glowed and inhaled deeply.

"Relax, Mr. Henry," she said. "The night is young. Enjoy your drink." She patted a seat beside her on the davenport and Rush sat down turning half toward her. "How are your articles coming?" she asked. It was an artless question asked in a very off-hand manner. Rush answered in the same manner.

"Fine," he said.

"How long will they take you?"

"It's hard to tell. It depends on how many I decide to write. It could be another week, it might be twice that."

"I'd like to read them. An outsider's view of Forest City should be interesting."

"I'll show you the final drafts," said Rush.

"They're pretty rough right now." He finished his drink and put it down on the coffee table. Gay drained hers and stood up.

"You are certainly impatient to be gone, young man," she said. "I lure you into my apartment and ply you with liquor and all the time you're champing at the bit to be gone. So we'll go." She reached for a wrap that hung over a chair and handed it to Rush.

"Leave us take things in order and at the time appointed," said Rush. He put the wrap around her shoulders. "I should do the luring and the plying and the time will come."

"What time?" asked Gay.

"The time for luring and plying. Come on; Carlo's won't be the same without us." He added privately that it would probably never be the same again without them.

Rush had kept his cab and it took them to Carlo's. The hands of Rush's watch read ten-fifteen as they entered. The waiter took them to the table Rush had reserved that afternoon. Across the room Matt Pedrick waved at them. At his side Kit English looked up and nodded without too much enthusiasm. Rush ordered drinks and took Gay to the dance floor while waiting for them. After the dance they returned to the table to find Pedrick waiting for them.

"Evening, children," he said. "Is this an item or

are you two just doing research for Mr. Henry's articles?"

"Oh, please don't put it in your paper, Mr. Pedrick," begged Gay. "Mr. Henry's wife and five children would·just die."

"My," said Pedrick looking at Rush, "prolific, isn't he? Didn't know you were a family man."

"I'm not. At least I wasn't."

Pedrick turned to look at Gay.

"Well, he acts like a father to me. You can't blame me for being fooled."

"Touché," said Pedrick.

"Touché," answered Rush. "But then, she reminded me so much of a maiden aunt of mine that I have to think twice or I'll remind her to take her liver pills."

"Touché, you louse," said Gay.

Pedrick opened his mouth to laugh aloud and suddenly closed it.

"That's funny," he said.

"I thought so too," said Rush.

Gay had followed Pedrick's eyes.

"He doesn't mean your nasty crack, you boor. He means what just came in."

"What came in?" asked Rush.

Pedrick spoke to Rush but his eyes followed two men around the edge of the room to the bar.

"A couple of guys who never come in here. Card Sully's two right hand men."

"Is Mr. Sully a freak, with two right hands yet?" asked Rush.

"Ha ha," said Gay. "That Chicago humor is excruciating."

"I forgot that you are a non-native," said Pedrick. "It's nothing really outlandish except that those two guys never come here. They're always at Sully's place. Of course," he added, "Sully's place is out of order at the moment. Maybe they're just relaxing. On vacation as it were and seeing what the other boys are doing."

"This is all very interesting," said Rush, "and no doubt it fascinates the habitués of this dive. Me, I have a call to make." He stood beside his chair. "Will you entertain Clara Bow here till I get back." He left the table before Gay could throw the glass she picked up.

He walked to the back of the room and followed the path toward the bar taken by the two men who had so interested Pedrick. The room was crowded and he had to force his way through slow moving masses of people. He seemed in no hurry. In fact he stopped almost dead still several times. Each time he reached in his pocket and did something to a small object he held in his two hands. Then he dropped it to the floor only to hurry on several yards and repeat the performance. He stopped at the bar for a quick straight shot of rye and returned to the table. Pedrick looked up.

"That was a short call," he said.

"Hardly worth making," said Rush. "The line was busy."

He sat down and picked up the drink Pedrick had ordered in his absence. As he drank the band stopped playing and the M.C. walked out onto the small square of floor to start the floor show. A spot centered on him and he raised his hand for silence. He got it for about ten seconds. Then a murmur started on the far side of the room. It grew till the M.C. looked angrily in that direction and stopped talking. The murmur grew and with the murmur came the noise of chairs being shoved back from the tables and angry voices began to be heard over the murmur. A door beside the bar opened and a tall dark man with broad shoulders came out. He looked in the direction of the disturbance. He looked for a moment then moved purposefully toward the center of it.

Pedrick looked puzzled.

"I wonder what the hell—" he started, then he sniffed. He breathed in deeply through his nostrils. Rush sniffed. Gay sniffed. Something was dead. Either that or an army of skunks had visited Carlo's. The smell caught in the air conditioning and spread around the room. It was overpowering.

"I'm a son of a—," said Pedrick, "a stink bomb. I wonder—" He stopped in mid sentence. "This is news," he said. "Be seeing you." He was out of his chair and gone in a flash.

"I don't think I can stand much more of this," said Gay, her handkerchief to her nose. "Let's get out of here."

"Just a minute," said Rush. "This is like old times in Chicago. I'd like to see what they do. Any way, you'd play hell getting out of here right now." He pointed to the doorway where a mass of people stampeded the check room in an effort to get out.

Rush looked to the bar. Only one of the two men were there now. The tall dark man walked up to the other one and spoke to him. Across the width of the room Rush could tell that his words were angry ones. The other man held up a hand and answered. A moment later his companion came back to join him and the three of them spoke together, the tall dark man looking at them from under heavy brows. Rush looked back at the mob struggling to get out and in its midst saw one figure struggling to get in. It was Carney. He broke away from the mass and stalked angrily across the floor to the three men at the bar. Rush watched as the same scene repeated itself. Then from the crowd cam another late entry. Card Sully broke through the crowd and came across the room to stand beside Carney. That was all Rush wanted to see. He was also becoming conspicuous for his failure to leave. He took Gay by one arm and led her to the now thinning crowd at the exit. They were in the fresh air outside before he spoke.

"I've been in glue factories that smelt like a rose compared to that," he said.

"What was it?" asked Gay.

"Pedrick guessed it," he said. "A stink bomb. I've smelled them before. They were quite the thing in Chicago at one time. If you didn't want to be protected you got a stink bomb from the protective association. A neat trick."

"But why should anybody drop a stink bomb in Carlo's?"

"Maybe they thought he needed protection," said Rush.

They finally maneuvered a cab out of the line in front of the night club and opened all the windows. The wind blew away all vestiges of the smell before they reached Gay's apartment.

"Is it luring time?" she asked as they reached the door of her apartment.

"And plying time. I will ply you with your liquor. To the extent of one drink, that is."

"Just one?" asked Gay.

"Just one."

Gay opened the door of the apartment and walked ahead of Rush into the living room. She allowed him to take off her wrap and turned to face him.

"I'm an understanding woman, Henry," she said. "I know you have business to do. I don't know what the hell you're up to, but you're up to something and it obviously takes time. But some time you're going to have to spend some time with me alone and you know it. So make your plans. Now ply me with that drink."

Rush poured drinks and they drank in silence. Then Rush stood up.

"Come here," he said.

She came and stood in front of him.

"Look," he said. "I'm very glad you are an understanding woman. I am up to something and it takes time. And sometime I'm going to spend some time with you alone. My plans are all made. In the meantime let's not ask questions. Let us eat, drink and be merry or a reasonable facsimile of the same."

"Roger," she said.

He put his hands on her shoulders then and pulled her to him. It was as before. Passion without urgency. Peace with a promise of ecstasy. And the softest lips within memory.

Rush left then with no backward glance and walked through the dim hall to the entranceway. There he stopped to look at a figure he had penciled on the back of an old envelope.

In the street he walked four blocks north, three west and a half north again. There he found a sheltering clump of bushes and crouched behind them, his eyes on the entrance of a large new house standing some fifty feet back from the street. Once he took a gun from his pocket and examined the load. Satisfied he returned the gun and resumed his vigil. A half hour passed and the muscles of his legs cramped. He half rose to stretch them when an automobile turned the corner south of him and swept up to stop beside the house Rush had watched. A man stepped out of the back seat, leaned in to speak to someone in the front seat and turned to walk toward the house. The car gathered momentum in a rush and was a half block away by the time the man was halfway to the house.

Rush stood up behind the bushes and pointed his gun at the man. He pulled the trigger three times in fast succession and turned and ran with all his might. He was eight blocks away in fifteen minutes having twisted and turned through alleys and gardens and back yards. Breathing heavily he slowed to a walk which took him ten minutes later into the lobby of his hotel. In his room he poured a drink of rye and grinned at his reflection in the mirror. He thought that suspicion should really be rife now. Card Sully would look twice at anyone who might possibly have shot at him. Card Sully of course would never know that the shots had come from blank cartridges.

Rush sat on the edge of his bed and picked up the phone. He gave the operator a number in Chicago and lit a cigarette while he waited. His call was through before the cigarette was half smoked, and a familiar voice helloed him.

"Hello, Pappy," he said. "Glad I caught you at home."

"Are you still alive?" asked Pappy.

"And well," said Rush. "I need some help, though."

"Who do you want?"

"You'd better send Smoky. Tell Gertrude to send Merwin. Tell her to tell him to mind Smoky till he gets here. Also I'd like one other. Ask Jim Todd at Continental if he can let me have Duffy for a few days. He's worked for me before. Gertrude will give the boys some dough and I'll take care of them after they get here."

"When do you need them?"

"Better have them fly. I can use them right away."

"They'll be in at five tomorrow afternoon then." Pappy paused a moment. "How are you doing?"

"Okay."

"Is it getting hot?"

"Not for me, yet. Some of the locals are burning a little."

"What's this killing I get on the AP wire?"

"That's one of the larger guns here. I haven't figured it yet. It could be anything. It worries me a little."

"Anything I can use yet?"

"Not yet, but Smoky can file anything he thinks you'll want. I've got an in with the local press now and they'll take care of pix if anything phenomenal breaks."

"Okay. Did you get my package?"

"I got and passed it on."

"That must have been a panic. Where did you use the bombs?"

"In a joint. It belongs to one of the bigger of the big shots here."

"That should make you real popular."

"I'm not trying to be the most popular man in Forest City. Just the oldest."

"I hope you make it. Good-bye, Rush. I'll have the boys there tomorrow afternoon."

"Thanks, Pappy. See you."

Rush hung up then and went to bed. He slept a full ten hours with a sleep that guaranteed the purest of consciences. The only thing was that he dreamed of red hair.

Chapter 9

The group that met shortly after five in Rush's hotel room was conglomerate to use the kindest adjective. Smoky, his usual striped shirt bulging over a belt that drooped a good city block below his navel. It's collar was loose as always and held in approximate place only by a stringy tie of indeterminate hue. He was the perfect picture of the guy who stands next to you at a neighborhood bar and talks about the state of the world. His appearances were deceptive. Smoky was a grade A, first run reporter. He knew his business and in his unorthodox way managed to do a hell of a job.

Smoky sat on the bed. In a straight chair by the window, staring at nothing particular sat Merwin. Merwin always stared and never at anything in particular. Merwin's value lay in an indestructible loyalty to Rush and an ability to follow orders to the letter, never more, never less. He also had the self effacing knack of shadowing. In this he was an artist.

Hunched in an arm chair in a corner sat a small nondescript man of an unguessable age. Duffy might be thirty and he might be fifty. The detective business to him was a job. He did his share of it very well, leaving brilliant deduction for someone else and handling the routine that would have stopped the brilliant deducer. He was a trained craftsman with a craftsman's pride in his work. He was also a likeable little guy and Rush had borrowed him from Continental several times before.

Robin Twist leaned against the door frame of the entrance to the bathroom. The fifth man in the room was Rush who stood at the dresser pouring from a dark brown bottle into a row of glasses. He turned to his guests.

"Pick them up yourselves. If you want anymore pour it yourself. I'm going to be busy talking."

"Again?" asked Smoky who already had his glass in his hand.

"And for some time," said Rush. "This is quite a caper and it needs some explaining." He took a long drink from his own glass and waited till they were all back in their seats.

"This is the way it stands. I've been hired to clean this town up. Take my word for it it needs it. You'll notice some things as you get around that will curl your hair. The trouble is that the people who live here, the voters, that is, don't know they need a clean-up. There's never any trouble so they just keep right on electing the guys who've always been in. The surface is neat and clean and that's enough for them. What they don't know is that they're paying about twice too much taxes. They don't know that every time the city buys something it pays almost double price. If it builds something it costs half again more than it should. They also don't know that an unbelievable amount of money is laid on the line in some of the shadiest gambling layouts you ever saw. They get away with murder here. You won't believe it. No house odds for them. The house bets a cinch every time it bets. They don't know that so they keep right on like a herd of sheep, or is it a flock of sheep."

"Flock," said Robin from the door.

"Okay, flock. What they need—"

"Don't tell me," said Smoky, "let me guess. What they need is some trouble. Some very special trouble of the post-war Henry brand."

"Hand that man seven silver dollars," said Rush. "That's exactly what they need and exactly what they're going to get. As a matter of fact that's what they're already getting."

"You haven't been loafing?" asked Smoky.

"No." said Robin. "He's been promoting. He's acquired the neatest redhead I've ever seen."

"That's routine," said Smoky. "But what's he been doing beside that?"

Robin held up his hand with the fingers spread. He ticked his fingers as he enumerated.

"He is at present guilty of assault and battery, vandalism, discharging a firearm within the city limits, and contributing to the delinquency of an adult. I'm speaking of that very adult looking redheaded chick if you're in doubt. What a career that would be, contributing to her delinquency."

"That firearm wouldn't be the one that knocked off this Marr I read about in the papers, would it?" asked Smoky.

"No," said Rush, "it wouldn't. That is a mystery to me. I wish to hell I knew who had done it. It was a big help to me but it may be very embarrassing before I'm through. Mr. Twist is being facetious about some blank cartridges I fired at Card Sully last night."

"I thought Holloween was a couple of days away yet," said Smoky.

"That was no prank, son. That was aimed at scaring the bejesus out of Mr. Sully."

Smoky got up and refilled his glass.

"I think I get it," he said. "The pitch is to set the various local thugs against each other until they start making a noise like gangs."

"Right, and if they don't make the noise, we will."

"This is going to be exciting. Duffy, did you bring your box of pineapples?"

"I never use them, Smoky," said the little man. "I'm a tommygun man myself. I got it from my father. He was with Dion O'Bannion."

"Okay, comedians," said Rush. "Settle down. This is the deal. Listen carefully, Merwin."

"Huh, whadja say, Rush?" Merwin's head came up as though someone had jerked a spring. His voice was hoarse, the result of many a glove laid ungently on his adam's apple. Merwin had fought in his youth, not wisely and not well.

"I said, 'listen carefully.' I want you to get this."

"Sure, Rush. I gotcha. I'll listen."

"Okay. For a couple days, at least for the next twenty-four hours, I want you to circulate around town. Hit the bars, the horse joints, the beaneries. Meet a lot of people. Act tough but don't start anything. Keep out of trouble but act like you knew something. Hint that you're from Chicago. Give the idea that you're gangsters somebody's brought in to do a job for them. Don't mention any names. I want both of the two bosses left to think the other guys are doing the importing. Stay away from cops, and stay away from each other. Just stir things up as much as you can and let the word get back to Carney and Sully that somebody is hiring gorillas from Chi." He looked at Merwin. "Got it, Merwin?"

"Sure, Rush. I'm a torpedo from Chicago. I'm hired by somebody here in this town, only I don't say who. I act tough. I stay away from—"

"Cops," finished Rush. "And don't actually say you're hired by anybody. Just hint at it."

"Okay, Rush. I'll make it a good one."

"Good for you, Merwin. You'd better plan to meet here tomorrow night about ten. I'll have some more stuff for you then."

They left then all except Robin.

"Anything for me?" he asked.

"You might keep an eye on Merwin," said Rush.

"I might also keep an eye on you. You're sitting in a very hot seat, friend. It might not hurt to have me fifty feet behind you for a while."

"Not yet. I don't think it's gone that far yet. I'm safe for a while yet."

"Like a virgin in a harem you are."

"You go play gangster for a while. I'll be all right."

"You're the boss," said Robin. "Watch it." He left the room then and Rush put on his coat and followed him ten minutes later. He headed for the *Chronicle* office and Bill Prime. He wanted some information on the reform candidate for mayor. The time was come to meet that gentleman and tell him fate was about to tap him on the shoulder. Mr. W. C. Covington, Rush had gotten his name from a campaign poster, was about to be visited by destiny.

He found Prime in his office and stated his mission.

"I think we'd better have Pedrick in. He knows more about people in this town than they know about themselves."

Rush was hesitant.

"Won't that involve telling him my innermost secrets?"

"I think you'd better expect that anyway. In

the first place he is one smart guy and if I start slanting news, he'll catch it in two editions. In the second place he can do a lot of good along that line in his column. You'd be amazed at how religiously people read it and how oracle-like they consider it. Pedrick can tell no lies. George W. was not in it with him."

Rush gave in then and Prime phoned for Pedrick who came into the office. Rush let Prime tell him the story. Pedrick sat it out in an unaccustomed silence. When Prime was through he looked at Rush.

"You know, my secretive friend, I suspicioned you from the first. You didn't look like an article writer to me. They wear glasses and ask dull questions. Your questions are far from dull and they never even remotely touch upon such article-like subjects as economics and population trends and such stuff."

Rush grinned at him.

"I tried," he said. "Next time I'll be more dull."

"It'll be an effort, I'm sure." Rush nodded his acceptance of the compliment. "Now, what can I do for you?"

Prime explained Rush's idea about slanting news. Pedrick got it at once and was enthusiastic.

"Propaganda fascinates me. Ever since I read Dale Carnegie I've had an uncontrollable yen to influence somebody. My time has come."

"You can influence people to your heart's content," said Rush. "I'll give you some ammunition daily. Right now I want a word about the life and times of one W. C. Covington. I'm going to approach him this afternoon."

"Willie?" said Pedrick. "A nice guy. Comparatively harmless but with a strong civic conscience. He's got a pretty thick hide or he wouldn't expose himself to the beating he's going to take."

"Want to bet?" asked Rush.

Pedrick looked at him through narrowed eyelids.

"Are you considering tampering with the ballot boxes?" he asked.

"Not at all. I'm going to elect him mayor by the will of the people."

"You," said Pedrick, "talk like a man with a paper head. My uncle's horse has just as good a chance as he has."

"I'll take bets," said Rush. "Look. While you are busy influencing Carney and Sully and their boys into thinking that they're at each other's throats, you'll be influencing the common people into thinking the same thing. I'm convinced that there are enough unenlightened common people in Forest City to swing the election once they get the word."

"What word is that?" asked Pedrick. "Could I hear it?"

"You can. The word is that they have been taken

for a municipal ride like nobody I ever heard of ever got taken for before. Beyond that their fair city has been a profitable plaything for a group of selfish, evil, grasping men for many years. When they find that out they aren't going to like it. They are even going to do something about it. Like electing Mr. W. C. Covington."

Pedrick shook his head.

"It's a dream," he said. "Maybe you can sell your bill of goods. I doubt it. But if you can, power to you. You may count me as one of your loyal supporters. And, brother, if you put it over make that read lifetime admirers."

"You're in," said Rush. "Now about W. C."

"Okay. Fiftyish, independently wealthy, wife and two kids of high school age, upright, member of the First M. E. Church, pillar of conservative society, and a pretty nice guy."

"Any guts?" asked Rush.

"Unknown quantity. Maybe if pushed enough."

"How far has he been pushed?"

"Figure it out for yourself. He doesn't have to run for Mayor. He knows it's a losing battle yet he sticks his chin out. There must be something there."

"Good," said Rush. "I'll push him the rest of the way. Where can I find him?"

Pedrick looked at his watch.

"At this moment he should be in office in the

Exchange Building. All he does there anymore is clip coupons but he keeps the office open. As a matter of fact I think it is now his campaign headquarters."

"Thanks, Matt," said Rush. "I think maybe he's my man. I'll give him a quick trial run."

Rush bypassed a pair of secretaries busy doing nothing and a roomful of people unenthusiastically addressing envelopes. The feeling of uselessness was heavy in the room. He found Mr. Covington seated behind a desk looking out of his window at the streets of residential Forest City spread out beyond the business district that lay directly below. He introduced himself. Mr. Covington was glad to see him but obviously curious about his reason for being there. Rush was very direct.

"Why do you want to be mayor, Mr. Covington?" he asked.

"You're not a resident of Forest City, are you?" asked Covington.

Rush shook his head.

"If you were you'd understand. I'm very fond of this city. I grew up here and I made what money I have here. My children are going to spend their lives here. I want it to be the kind of city they can be proud of. I want to be proud of it myself. It isn't that kind of city. If you lived here you'd know how far it misses being the kind of place you can be proud of."

"All right," said Rush. "How strongly do you want to be Mayor?"

"I should think that would be obvious. I'm spending a good deal of money and more time. I'm bucking a machine that's old in intrigue and practical politics. Isn't that an answer?"

"That's one kind of answer," said Rush. "It didn't quite answer my question. Let me be hypothetical for a moment. If it were possible to guarantee your election would you countenance certain activities that might not look too well in the cold light of day? In other words are the means or the end more important to you?"

Covington swung full around in his chair to face Rush.

"I think you'll have to qualify that hypothesis. You sound very much like somebody who wants something. What is it?"

"You're quite right, Mr. Covington. I'll qualify and expand. I'll even lay my cards on the table. I am a private detective from Chicago. I once managed to clean up a city that was almost as bad as Forest City. Someone has engaged me to do the same thing for Forest City. To me, it looks like the easiest and most permanent way would be to elect you mayor. That is what I propose to do. But only on one condition."

"Which is?"

"That you accept my advice as to how to keep

it clean. Reform Mayors are a dime a dozen. Only one in a hundred really reforms anything. I don't want to go to the trouble of electing you only to have you let things slide as much as they are now."

Covington looked at him very curiously.

"You have a strange faculty for making very extraordinary statements sound ordinary, Mr. Henry. How do you propose to elect me?"

"That should be obvious," said Rush. "Your biggest handicap is the fact that almost nobody realizes what a hell of a state things are in Forest City. You can talk to them for a thousand years and it'll be just that, talk. I propose to show them. I have already started as a matter of fact. You may not know it but there is a gang war going on in Forest City. The gangs don't even know it yet, but they will. You see, the odd thing about your bosses in Forest City is that they don't look, act, or sound like bosses. There is no strife, nothing. They are too well organized. So I'll fix it so they sound like bosses. I've almost got them at each other's throats now. In a day or so Joe Public, Forest City brand, is going to think hell has popped in his town. If I can help it no one will get hurt. It'll be sound and fury with no body blows struck, only I'm afraid it won't be quite that clean. Somebody's going to get hurt, I hope it's only those who have it coming but an innocent bystander may get caught before I'm through."

Covington had sat silently through Rush's long speech. He looked at his hands lying flat on the desk for a long moment before he spoke.

"Who hired you to come here?"

Rush shook his head.

"I don't know. I was retained by a highly respected firm of lawyers in Chicago. My client prefers to remain anonymous. The lawyers will pay me when and if I'm through."

"And what is my alternative. What will you do if I fail to cooperate?"

"Oh, I'll elect you anyway probably. The difference will be that I'll sic the boys on each other till they run each other out of business. It'll be nastier that way but surer unless I have complete cooperation from you after you are elected."

"You don't leave me much choice."

"I didn't intend to," said Rush. "I just wanted to look you over and see if you were worth fighting for."

Covington smiled for the first time during the interview.

"What have you decided?" he asked.

"I think you'll do," said Rush.

"What do you want me to do now?"

"Nothing that you wouldn't do anyway. You'll recognize my ammunition as it appears. Use it. I would suggest a public statement by yourself that the gangs which have ruled Forest City are becoming unmanageable. Read your papers; you'll find things to point the finger of shame at in quantity. I'll give you more to back up anything you want to say about Carney and Sully."

Covington took a deep breath.

"All right, Henry. If I'm elected Mayor I'll listen to you. In the meantime I don't want to know anything you are doing. I want to be completely disassociated from you. You go your way and I'll go mine and you come see me after the election."

Rush smiled at him.

"You'll be a practical politician yet," he said. "You'll be seeing me." With that he left the office and returned to the *Chronicle* building.

Chapter 10

Tiring of looking for cabs Rush hired a car by the week and drove it on its maiden voyage as far as he was concerned to Gay Wimberly's apartment. They were invited to Pedrick's for drinks and a later trip to whatever seemed the logical place to go. Gay greeted him at the door with a drink.

"Put it down, sonny," she said. "We will blow at once. I'm not spending anymore time sitting around this apartment with you waiting for something to happen. Like you said, the time will come, but who knows when and I'm too young to wait."

Rush grinned, downed the drink and put his arms around her.

"The time is overdue for this," he said and kissed her quite thoroughly. He stopped quite suddenly and picked up Gay's wrap. It was becoming increasingly difficult to remain objective while kissing Gay. Something happened inside him that was very pleasant but extremely disturbing. He made a mental note to think about Gay, and about Gay and Rush Henry when he had time. It was a situation that required an attitude on his part and every time he thought he had one he kissed her again and there went his attitudes out the window.

He led the way to the car and they drove in

silence to Pedrick's apartment. He parked the car around the corner and took Gay's chin in his hand, looking in her eyes with an unstudied frown. It was a long moment. Then he bent quickly and kissed her again, quickly this time, allowing no time for the shattering of another attitude. He leaned across her and unlatched the door then went around the car to help her out.

Pedrick was waiting for them at the door. Beyond him Rush saw Kit English sitting on a hassock, her dress spread around her in careful abandon.

"Welcome, youall," said Pedrick. "Pour your own and sit."

Rush poured drinks for himself and Gay. They sat on a low divan facing Pedrick who had seated himself on the chair behind Kit.

"What shall we do with time?" asked Pedrick. "Shall we carouse or shall we burden the hours with what the ancients used to call 'good conversation'?"

"My wants are simple," said Rush. "Just a house by the side of the road and an unlimited supply of rye whiskey. How about a little of both?"

"Houses and whiskey?" asked Pedrick.

"No," said Rush. "Carousing and conversation."

"Okay, let's talk. What do you know enough about to feel superior discussing?"

"I'm a great hand to talk about life."

"It's done. I will now tell you about life." Pedrick took a long drink from his glass. "Everybody gets one. After that it's up to him. Some people eat, drink and raise a family. That's fine. I don't know what we'd do if our supply of people like that ran out. They have no violent urges. They fight no public battles, and they never want what somebody else has got."

"That's a hundred of the hundred thirty million," said Rush. "Tell us about the other thirty million, Mr. Anthony."

"They are the people with built-in urges. Twenty-nine million of them are not otherwise equipped to do anything about their urges. The other million make a stab at it. A few of them get the job done."

"But not always the same job," said Rush.

"You are an understanding man, Mr. Henry," said Pedrick. "No, not always the same job. Some of them write books, others build bridges or run corporations or just sit and gather money."

"And some of them just sit and gather power. That is the most virulent urge of them all."

"You amaze me, Henry." Pedrick was semi-serious. "I never thought of you as a philosopher. You're more the man of action type."

"I'm a split personality. And which of these would you say was the happiest? The hundred million or the thirty million, or even the few who get the job done?"

"I don't think happiness enters in where the guys

with the urges are concerned. They're never completely happy because they are never completely satisfied—which is a kind of happiness in itself."

"That's a little obscure but I think I get it. This lack of fulfillment is a kind of happiness in that there's always another battle to fight and the pleasure is in the fighting, not the winning."

"Exactly. I think I'll cultivate you, Henry. There's more to you than meets the eye."

"There's plenty of both of you meeting the ear," said Kit. "If this is your idea of conversation I'll take a quiet evening with the Encyclopedia Britannica."

"Do we bore you?" asked Pedrick.

"Did you ever see a woman who wasn't bored when somebody else was doing the talking?" asked Gay.

Pedrick looked at Rush and shook his head in deep mock sorrow.

"We've lost them somewhere. I was about to expound the virtues of Nietzche's Superman but I'll hold that till later."

"Maybe you two can steal a moment alone some time. You and Superman." Kit stood up on that line. "Let's go someplace. I'd like to hear a little uneducated noise."

"I wonder if Carlo's is deodorized?" asked Rush.

"I don't know. There was a rumor today that Jimmy Fidler flew in with a B-29 full of Arrid."

Pedrick snapped his fingers. "Now, why did I waste that on you. It's a natural for the column."

"You can use it tomorrow," said Kit. "Come on, let's go."

Carlo's was not doing what could be called a rushing business. There were areas of as much as three or four tables entirely empty. Rush grinned an inner grin. That was hitting where it hurt. Where the money comes in. A waiter showed them to a table and took their order for drinks. The drinks came and with them the floor show. The M.C. was very jolly and the acts effervescent but somehow nobody's heart seemed in it. The crowd tried hard to enjoy themselves but it missed somehow. The lights went up after the floor show and the band began playing for dancing.

Kit and Pedrick got up to dance, Pedrick under protest, stating that he was not the type and besides he was too old. As they left the table Gay looked at Rush.

"I'm not going to twist your arm, Nijinski, but are you going to dance with me?" she asked.

"Yes," said Rush. "I'm looking forward to it very much. Let me finish my drink."

He raised the glass to his lips and looked over the rim as he drank. Across the room leaning against the wall, looking anywhere but at Rush stood Robin Twist. As he stood there he idly buffed the fingernails of his right hand against his coat lapel. It was an old signal. It meant, see me right away. Rush put down his glass.

"This is no gag," he said, "but I have to see a man. It won't take long."

Gay sighed resignedly and beckoned to a waiter. "I'll get drunk while you're gone."

Rush left the table and walked past Robin and into the men's room. It was almost empty. A moment later Robin came in and began to wash his hands. Rush came to stand beside him and wash. The only other occupant of the room left and Robin spoke over the flow of water in the bowl.

"It's working," he said.

Rush raised his eyebrows at Robin's reflection in the mirror.

"Nobody knows what's happening but they know something's happening. They're getting edgy and a lot of the boys are wearing rods. That's new in this town."

"Yeah," said Rush. "Anything else?"

"Nobody puts it in words but they're beginning to wonder if Carney and Sully are getting along as well as they used to. That's one school of thought. The other is that maybe somebody from outside is trying to move in. I'm surprised nobody ever did. What a gravy train."

"You can say that again. Have you seen any of the boys?"

"Smoky was playing poker in a house game downtown when I went through. I kibitzed awhile and heard him twist the knife a couple of times. He's very good at it."

Rush dried his hands.

"Keep pitching," he said. "I've got a new angle for tomorrow. I'll give it to you tomorrow night at ten. Have all the boys in my room."

"Roger," said Robin.

Rush went back to the table then and stood beside Gay.

"Come on, Pavlova," he said. "On your feet."

Gay danced as Rush had known she would. Expertly, and as if this were a new experience that they had found together. It was dancing with the difference that they were doing it and not somebody else. She made it a very personal thing and pleasant. The music stopped and as if it were the most natural thing in the world Rush took her hand and held it in his as they walked to the table.

Kit and Pedrick were there before them and as they sat down Max Carney loomed up behind Kit's chair and beamed down at them.

"Everything all right?" he asked.

"Just fine, Max," said Pedrick. "Sit down and have a drink."

"These are on me," said Carney. He raised a finger and a chair appeared out of nowhere. He sat down and a waiter materialized to take their orders. "I'm glad you came tonight, Matt," he said. "I'd appreciate it if you'd give me an item in your column on last night. I want to explain what happened."

"I'd like to know myself," said Pedrick.

"It was some trouble in the air conditioning system. Some of the cooling fluid leaked into the air ducts. I wish you'd give that a line in the paper. I don't want anybody to think it could happen again."

"I'll put it in tomorrow, Max," said Pedrick.

"It's a good story," said Rush. "But I'll make you a bet."

Carney let his head turn slowly to look at Rush.

"On what?" he asked.

"I'll bet two to one that you found some splinters of glass on the floor across the way."

Carney's eyes narrowed.

"What makes you think we did?"

"I've smelled that smell before. That was no cooling fluid, that was a stink bomb stink. I'd know it anywhere."

"I don't think I'd mention that to anyone else if I were you, Henry," said Carney.

"I wasn't thinking of mentioning it," said Rush. "You've got a good story. I'd hate to spoil it."

"I'd hate to have you." Carney looked at him speculatively. "You know, I'd hate to have you get the wrong idea of this town, Henry. I wouldn't want you to think that the things that have happened since you came are typical. We don't allow things like that in this town."

"I'm sure you don't," said Rush wondering if he was being warned.

He didn't wonder long.

"No," said Carney. "When we have troubles like these we do something about them. It usually turns out that the trouble is all for the one who started it."

"Anybody'd be foolish to buck a setup like yours," said Rush. Let him figure that out, he thought.

A figure appeared at Carney's shoulder and informed him that he had a phone call from his wife. He excused himself and left the table.

Pedrick yawned.

"Interesting character," he said.

"Very," said Rush.

Pedrick yawned again.

"To hell with it," he said. "I'm tired. Let's go, Kit."

They had driven two cars so Kit and Pedrick left alone. Rush and Gay had another drink and decided to go. As Rush was helping Gay into the car he remembered what had seemed unusual about the evening.

"Look," he said. "It just occurred to me. Don't you work anymore? This is the third night in a row you've been out with me. Don't tell me you're giving up everything for Henry."

"No," said Gay, "I just have a new job. I've been meaning to tell you."

"Fine. What are you doing now?"

"This'll kill you. I'm working for Max Carney."

"Doing what, for God's sake?"

"That's the part that will kill you. I'm keeping an eye on you."

Chapter 11

Rush looked at her for a moment, a long moment, then let the car into gear and drove off.

"That has its advantages," he said.

"Yes, I don't have to work very hard and the pay is excellent."

"I'll see to it that you work harder, my love," said Rush. "I hope you enjoy it."

"I'm sure I will."

Rush turned at the tone of her voice and Gay was smiling at him from the dimness of the car. He smiled back at her.

"Jezebel," he said.

"I'm a bad girl," she agreed.

"How did Carney get ahold of you?"

"Didn't you know? He owns the Blue Goose. I just changed jobs not employers."

"Did he explain why he wanted me watched?"

"No, except that you were a stranger and a reporter. He wanted a line on what you were writing."

"In that case I'll have to write something right away so you can tell him about it."

"At least tell me something to tell him. I want him to think I'm earning my money."

As Rush braked to a stop at Gay's apartment

house he thought of something that probably hadn't occurred to Gay. It was on his mind as he followed her to her apartment. She mixed him a nightcap and he drank slowly, deep in thought.

"Look, Gay," he said finally. "You'd better not make up things about my writing to feed to Carney. He's liable to find out I'm not writing and he doesn't like people to fool him."

"No," said Gay as seriously as Rush, "he doesn't. What would you suggest that I tell him?"

"Tell him exactly what I do do. So far you haven't seen me do anything he wouldn't like. There may be a few things I'd want you to forget but I'll warn you about those."

"Okay," said Gay. "Now, if a girl isn't too forward, could she ask what the hell you are doing here if you're not writing."

"You can ask," said Rush after a moment's silence, "but I doubt if you'll find out. I'm not sure I want you to know yet."

Gay set her drink down on the table and came to stand directly in front of Rush.

"Why, you nameless name," she said furiously. "You obscenity as Mr. Hemingway would say. I tell you everything and you don't trust me with anything. You louse," she added bitterly.

Rush held up a hand flat for a moment then lowered it to her shoulder.

"Hold it, Gay," he said. "Take it easy. I trust you

fine. What I meant was that I was afraid it might not be safe for you if you knew."

Gay looked at him suspiciously.

"I'll take a chance on that," she said. "Come on, tell mother. What are you doing as if I couldn't guess."

"Guess," said Rush.

"You're trying to run Sully and Carney and Gunn and Carver out of town. I don't know why but damned if I don't think you are."

"That's a good guess. That's approximately what I'm doing. I'm doing it because I get paid for it."

"By whom for heaven's sake?"

Rush told her as much of the story as he wanted her to know. It took another drink to make it. When he was through he set down an empty glass.

"How long do you estimate this will take, Mr. Henry?" asked Gay.

"Not long the way things are going."

"Do you think you'll have to kill anyone else?"

"You mean Marr?" Rush grinned. "I didn't kill Mr. Marr. Somebody did me that favor. One more favor like that and the job'd be almost done."

"I'll see if I can't arrange it," said Gay. "Then maybe you could spend a little time with me without your mind being a couple blocks away."

Rush looked at her and his smile was slightly forced.

"My big trouble is keeping my mind off you when I'm a couple blocks away."

Gay's eyes became very big.

"Why, Mr. Henry. What you said."

"Yes," said Rush. "What I said. Also what I'll do if I stay here much longer."

"Is that bad?" asked Gay.

"No, it's swell but first things first, damn it."

"I'm going to do some tinkering with your idea of what things come first," said Gay. "We don't see eye to eye there."

Rush grinned and kissed her very quickly then he left without another word.

In the car he drove slowly, thinking. The fact that Carney had set Gay to watching him was interesting. It needed thought. Only half consciously he turned left in the direction of Sully's house. The chances were good that Carney held high suspicions of him. There were too many coincidences for a man as smart as Carney to miss connecting him with the turn of things in Forest City. He'd have to take the gloves off soon. He made a turn to the right and drove three blocks slowing and parking fifty feet from the intersection in the shadows of a mammoth elm. Sully's house was a hundred feet north of the same intersection. Now might be the time to cast another stone in the troubled waters. He got out of the car and walked across the street to the shelter of bushes that edged the sidewalk around Sully's house. There was a light in the lower front room and he wanted a look inside before he made any move.

He made a cautious survey of the terrain and found it vacant. He took one step toward the house then halted and faded back into the bushes. A car whirled around the corner on two wheels and drew up with screaming breaks in front of Sully's house. The door of the house flew open and Sully came running down the steps throwing a topcoat around his shoulders. He got to the sidewalk and halfway across the parking when the silence fell apart in a sudden thunder of gunfire. From the open window of the car spits of flame shot at Sully. He stopped dead still for a moment, put out a hand toward the car, took a half step and fell. An arm reached out of the car and pumped two more shots into his body. Then the car roared away from the curb.

Rush didn't wait a second. Already lights were coming on in the neighborhood and doors were flying open. He turned on his heel and ran full tilt to his rented car. In a matter of seconds he was a block away. He drove fast for another block or two then slowed his pace to a respectable speed and finding no one in pursuit turned back toward town. He garaged the car in the hotel garage and went directly to his room. There he speedily undressed and got into bed.

Sleep was not easy to woo, nor did he try very hard. There was too much on his mind. When he finally relaxed it was with the conviction that somebody else was operating in Forest City with the same end as his in view. Operating, not for the same reason, but to the same end. He couldn't see Carney in the role, he was too smart and had too much to lose. His last thought before drifting to sleep was that it would be ironic indeed if his mythical Chicago gangsters had come to life and were truly trying to take over the town. It was logical enough. Forest City would be a neat plum, and ripe for the picking of the big city trouble boys.

When he awoke in the morning Smoky was sitting in his easy chair with a glass of his whiskey in his hand.

"Damn it," said Rush, "I wish you guys would stop picking my door lock, especially when I'm home."

"Do you want me to wake up the whole floor? I knocked twice but you were asleep and didn't hear me so I just eased in."

Rush got up and washed. He was busy shaving and Smoky came to stand in the door.

"Read the papers yet?" he asked.

"In my sleep?" asked Rush.

"You should. There's news."

"What's happened now? Did Sully get shot?"

"You guessing or do you know?"

"Guessing," said Rush shortly. "Did he?"

"Yeah, right in front of his house last night about two. Wife's statement says he got a phone call that his joint was burning down and that someone would pick him up. He ran out and somebody gunned him and drove away."

"Is that all they've got?"

"According to the papers that's the lid. I've got a cop I buy a drink for now and then. He says headquarters is a madhouse. These two shootings are the only crime they've had in this town in ten years and nobody knows what to do. They got cobwebs on all their investigation equipment. He's not even sure that anybody down there knows how to check ballistics. They may have to call in somebody to check Sully's slugs with Marr's."

"That'll be a nice item for the papers. The voters'll love it."

"Won't they. What are you going to do about it?"

"About what, the killings? Nothing. They're not my business."

"Got an alibi?"

Rush turned slowly till he was facing Smoky.

"Do I need one?"

"Not with me, chummy. But you might with the law. You'd be a neat way out of their troubles if they could stick them on you." He looked at

Rush closely. "Hey, why so jumpy? Do you need an alibi?"

Rush looked at him for a minute then slowly grinned.

"Yeah. I was there. In the bushes. I saw whoever it was let him have it."

"The hell. You're lucky you didn't get caught."

"Don't tell me. I'm still breathing hard."

"Don't let it get you down, Twist or I will alibi you if you need it. Just let us know."

"I'll think up a good one and set it with you. Call me or have Robin call me in an hour."

"Okay, anything else?"

"I want all you guys up here tonight at ten. I've got a deal cooking and I'll need some help."

"Okay. I'll lower the boom on the boys. See you tonight."

Smoky was gone as silently as he had come. Rush dressed slowly and lit a contemplative cigarette. Smoky had pointed a finger at a point he had overlooked. He didn't have an alibi for Marr's death either. It had happened while he was on his way to pick up Gay. Somebody else might pick it up and make something of it. He'd have to set an alibi quick.

He was right. His phone rang and he picked it up, stubbing out his cigarette in the tray beside the phone. The voice was slightly muffled as though intentionally disguised.

"Mr. Henry?" it asked.

"Speaking," said Rush.

"This is X. Do you know to whom I refer?"

"If you know a man named Leach in Chicago, I do."

"I know him. He offered you ten thousand dollars to do a job for me."

"I know you," said Rush. "I didn't expect to hear from you though."

"I didn't expect to have to call. However, your methods force me to get in touch with you."

"My methods?"

"The killing of Marr and Sully. I realized when I hired you that I was asking for violence but I didn't expect outright murder."

"Do I understand that you think I killed Marr and Sully?"

"I do. And it's got to stop."

"You're wrong and I doubt if it will. You don't have enough money. Mr. X, whoever you are, you don't have enough money if your name turns out to be Rockefeller to hire me to kill anybody. Let's get that straight right now. Whoever is shooting up your citizens is doing me a favor, it makes my job that much easier, but it isn't me."

"I didn't expect you to admit it. However, it must stop. If it doesn't I'll be forced to place what information I have in the hands of the police."

"Just what information do you have, Mr. X?" asked Rush.

"I'm fully aware of the fact that you have no alibi for either murder. Also the police will be interested to know that you were hired to clean up this town."

"You amaze me, X," said Rush. "I have alibis, very good ones. And while I'm at it let's clear up another point. I'm going to clean up your city. I'm going to do it my way. When I'm through I'm going to Leach and ask for ten thousand dollars. I expect to get it. If I don't I'll sue Leach and that'll smoke you out into the open. In the meantime don't sit around and stew about the killings. Those guys had it coming. They earned it years ago. If it'll make you feel better I'll dig around and find out who did kill them and throw it in with the original price. I like to give full value. Now, good-bye, Mr. X. It's been a pleasure meeting you."

Rush hung up then. He smiled at the telephone. It gave him a very nice feeling to have hung up on X since he was quite sure that X had intended to hang up on him.

Chapter 12

Rush had hardly replaced the phone when it rang again. It was Robin.

"Smoky says you might need a front for last night," he said.

"That isn't all. I just remembered I had a blank space in my diary at the time Marr was shot. Cover me for both of them, will you?"

"Sure. Where were we?"

"I met you just outside Pedrick's apartment house the night Marr was gunned and you rode downtown with me. We had business to talk over. I'm covered after that. Last night you waited for me outside Gay Wimberly's apartment and rode downtown with me. More business."

"What was that time last night?"

"From about one-thirty to two-thirty. We talked a lot."

"That's good. I'm clear for those times. I wasn't with anybody who could make a liar of me. Consider yourself alibied."

"Thanks."

"See you tonight at ten."

"Will do."

Rush ate a fast breakfast and went to the offices of the *Chronicle*. He had business with Bill Prime and he wanted a word with Pedrick. He found

Pedrick in his office, going over a batch of copy.

"What are the wild winds whispering about our Mr. Sully and his sudden demise?" asked Rush.

"It's a strange thing about that," said Pederick. "My sources are all dried up. It isn't that they won't talk, it's that they don't know anything to talk about."

"My sources," said Rush calmly appropriating Smoky's cop, "say that the law doesn't know anything either. I also have an angle for you."

Pedrick reached for a scratch pad.

"Give," he ordered.

"I'm told that the city department of police is so out of date that they don't have a ballistics man capable of comparing the bullets that killed Sully with those that killed Marr. The voters should know that. You could put in the form of a question, Winchellwise— 'what city police department et cetera?'"

"I could indeed. Anything else?"

"You might relay a random thought of mine."

"Which is?"

"Wouldn't it be too poetic if there really were outside gangsters moving in to take over the town?"

"Do you really believe that?"

"It might be. It fits all the facts. They operate that way."

Pedrick shook his head.

"I'd hate to see that. It'd be into the fire from the frying pan."

"Don't worry about them. If they're really here I'll scare them off. I have a few connections in Chicago that might do me some good here."

Pedrick looked up to see if he was joking. He decided he wasn't.

"I'll give the angle a play tonight."

"Say," said Rush. "There is something else. I have to talk to Bill Prime first, but if I sell him on a deal I'd like to use you and your car tonight. Kit and hers too if possible."

"I think I can arrange it. What've you got in mind?"

"I'll let you know after I talk to Prime."

"I'll hold myself at attention till I hear from you."

Rush left Pedrick's office then and walked through the city room to Prime's office. The white-haired editor was dictating. He waved Rush to a seat while he finished then dismissed his secretary and turned to face Rush. Rush stopped him before he could speak.

"No, I didn't kill Sully. I don't know who did. I wish I knew so I could thank him. I didn't kill Marr either. I have alibis to prove it."

"You wound me, boy. I wasn't going to accuse you. The idea had never occurred to me."

"It will. It's already occurred to my Mr. X. He

called to tell me to stop killing people."

"What did you tell him?" asked Prime.

"The same thing I told you and a few other well chosen words. I also intimated I had alibis."

"Do you?"

"I do now."

"Fine, now what's on your mind today?"

"I have a chore I want you to do as privately as possible."

"Anything within reason. What have you dreamed up now?"

Rush leaned across the desk and took a scratch pad and a pencil. As he spoke he sketched rapidly on the pad.

"I want a thousand posters about twelve by eighteen printed by ten-thirty tonight. I want something like this on them." He shoved the scratch pad across to Prime. It read as follows:

DO YOU KNOW WHAT IS HAPPENING
IN YOUR CITY?
The MACHINE which controls your city
is beginning to break up.
The men who run the machine are at war
with each other.
Outside gangsters are 'chiselling in'.
THE WORST IS YET TO COME!!!
There will be more shooting, more blood
shed, more violence.

IS THIS WHAT YOU WANT FOR
YOUR CITY?
REMEMBER YOU HAVE TO LIVE HERE.

"I want that set in as startling type as you can make it. I want to focus attention on what's going on in Forest City and you can't do that in the paper without trouble. Then when the things are up all over town you treat it as a news item and make it sound like there might be something in the charges. It'll start people talking and that's the only way you can win elections."

Prime nodded slowly.

"It's a good idea," he said. "I'd hate to get caught printing the damn things but I'll do it. I'll run them off myself on an old hand set press we never use anymore. The pressroom will be empty after eight and I can get them out in an hour or so."

"Okay, I'll pick them up myself at ten." Rush grinned. "I can see Carney's face when they turn up in the morning."

"How are you going to get them out?"

"I've got four men of my own in town and I'm borrowing several cars. Pedrick will help me. We'll start after everybody's in bed and plaster them all over the residential district. It shouldn't take over three or four hours. We can sleep late in the morning."

"Okay. Drive up to the rear entrance and I'll

hand them out to you."

"There'll be another little act going on about the same time or just afterwards. Keep your ears open and give it a play."

"Should I have a man anywhere?"

"No, it might leak. You'll get it soon enough anyway. It'll just point up the other story."

"I'll keep an eye open and I'll cover the poster story myself. I'll treat it editorially. It should be fun."

Rush left then and walked out of the door into the noon sunshine. He was looking down the street ahead of him for a restaurant sign when he began to notice a heavy afterbeat to the sound of his own footsteps. He listened for a few steps, then identified the sound. Someone was walking close behind him and slightly out of step with him. He turned as he walked and looked over his shoulder. There five feet behind him was Junior as big as life and twice as ugly. He looked over the other shoulder and there was Junior's pal. They increased their stride and walked beside him, one on either side.

"Good morning, boys," said Rush. "Did you come back for another lesson?"

Junior grunted offensively. His partner was more verbose.

"This is a short trip, chum," he said. "We're taking you to see a guy."

"Anybody I know?" asked Rush.

"You'll know him all right," said Junior.

"Quiet, Junior. Now, chum, are you gonna give us trouble or are you coming along like a good boy."

Rush considered. He didn't doubt his ability to get away from these two clowns in broad daylight on a crowded street. But two things deterred him. They seemed dim enough mentally to start shooting and he had an effection for innocent bystanders. Also, he thought it might be interesting to meet their boss on his own terms.

"No," he said, "no trouble. I'll be a good boy this time. Where are we going."

The smaller man held up a hand and by obvious prearrangement a car swung into the curb beside them. The back door swung open and Rush stepped in. Junior and his pal took seats on either side of him and the car moved off. It went through the business district and into a factory section stopping at last by a large warehouse. The smaller man opened the door and motioned to Rush.

"Out," he said.

Rush got out and was guided through a side door down a lane through cases of whiskey piled high to the ceiling. At the end of the lane he was motioned to the right and came up to a door with a sliding panel. Junior knocked and the panel slid open only to shut immediately. The door swung open and Rush was prodded through. He found himself in a neatly fitted ante room. His captors motioned him through the ante room to another door which opened on a more sumptuous office with a large mahogany desk behind which sat Max Carney. Carney looked up as he came through the door and motioned him to a chair. Junior and his pals took seats on either side of the door. Carney reached to a cabinet behind him and brought out a bottle of whiskey. Rush noted the lable and grinned. Carney was watching him carefully.

"I've investigated you very carefully, Henry. That bottle should prove it. I even know you prefer Old Overholt Rye whiskey."

Rush stood up and went to the cabinet behind Carney. There he found a glass. He opened the bottle and poured an inch in the glass. He drank it down and poured another long inch which he took around to his chair and sipped.

"I'm complimented, Carney," he said. "Why this unusual interest in me?"

"I also found that you are the kind of man who doesn't like to beat around the bush so let's not kid each other. All I want to know is how much."

Rush raised his eyebrows.

"How much what?" he asked.

"How much to lay off Forest City."

"You'll have to put that in easier words than that," said Rush. "I'm not with you."

"Okay," said Carney, "I'll spell it out. I dug up what you did in Weston. I used to know Nose

Gaust. I know that if you could knock him over you could cause me a lot of trouble. We're much better organized here than Nose was in Weston and I can take care of you if I have to. The only thing that really bothers me is why you're nosing in here. The only thing I can figure is that some reformer is paying you to blow the lid off. Okay. I'll pay you more."

"You ought to check your information a little," said Rush. "Whoever gave you the dope missed something."

Carney was honestly surprised.

"What did I miss?" he asked.

"They should have told you that I never sell out. Supposing I was here for the reason you say and that somebody was paying me, you haven't got enough money to buy me off. Nobody has."

"That's a little silly, Henry," said Carney. "I won't give you the old guff about every man having a price, but when it comes to a choice of your neck or a large chunk of dough, any man's going to think twice."

"Not any man and I'm not worried about my neck."

Carney's face was immobile. His eyes were rock hard.

"I'd start worrying about it."

Rush grinned a slow infuriating grin.

"Is that a threat, Maxie?" he asked.

"That," said Carney, "is a threat."

"Who's going to be after my neck, these two bit thugs you sent after me today?"

There was a deep growl behind Rush and Carney held up a hand.

"Don't you think they could take care of you?" he asked.

"No, and besides you're too smart to send them after me." He drained his whiskey and stood up. He lit a cigarette and flicked the match at the ash tray on Carney's desk. "Let me make a speech, Maxie," he said. "Let *me* issue a couple of threats. I'm going to run you out of town so far it'll take three weeks to reach you by cable. I'm going to bust up your neat little monopoly into such little pieces they'll think somebody split an atom in your lap. I'm going to do it in about one more week. You're licked, Carney. You're licked bad and you'll know it after the city elections next week. I'd start pricing tickets for Timbuctoo and figuring how much dough I could take with me." Rush stopped and looked around at Junior and his friend.

"As far as your dime store comics back there are concerned, let me leave you with this thought. If anything happens to me the Chicago *Express* will spend fifty thousand dollars finding out what. They'll give this town so much publicity you'll nevar dare show you face again. And one more thing, Maxie. I have a friend in town who worked with me in the war. He was one of Uncle Sam's smarter boys. We're very fond of each other and if I turn up missing he won't wait for the judge and jury; he'll shoot you like a dog and all your thugs won't help you. And while I'm at it I'd better warn your boys to be careful with those rods they're toting. If they should happen to knock over my friend you'd be in the same spot because I'd have to take care of you myself."

Rush walked toward the door till he stood between Junior and his friend.

"Sleep on it, Maxie," he said.

He turned, flipped ashes on Junior's lap and went out the door without a word said to stop him.

Chapter 13

It was quite an army that Rush mustered at three o'clock in the morning. He had picked up a thousand posters from Prime's own hands at the delivery door of the *Chronicle* several hours earlier and marshalled his crew at the back door of Pedrick's apartment house at three. They divided the posters and the crew among the three cars. Rush and Gay went in Rush's rented car. Smoky and Merwin who amused Pedrick greatly were in Pedrick's car and Robin and Duffy were in Kit English's car. Earlier, Rush, with the help of Pedrick, had mapped out the residential district in three sections and each car headed for a section.

Three hours later as the first glow of the sun faded the darker blue of the eastern night they met again in Pedrick's apartment. Pedrick opened a bottle of rye and poured heavy shots in highball glasses. He proposed a toast.

"To ourselves, of course. Hard liquor for hard men and damnation to the foe."

They drank and Rush looked thoughtfully at his glass.

"After that toast I feel as though I ought to smash this on the stone floor," he said.

"Smash ahead," said Pedrick, "but you'll clean it up."

"I've just reconsidered," he said. "I'm also dead on my feet. Let's to horse and away. Robin, you drive Kit's car to her house and I'll follow and pick you up. The rest of you call a cab."

In the alley behind Pedrick's where they had parked the car Rush and Robin held a brief conference following which they spent a moment smearing mud over the license plates of the two cars. Then Robin drove off with Rush and Gay close behind him. Out of the alley in the street Robin turned right.

"Does he know where he's going?" asked Gay. "That's not the way to Kit's house and she'll be needing her car in an hour or two."

"She'll get it in plenty of time," said Rush. "Just hang on, we're going for a little ride."

Robin's car picked up speed and headed through the residence districts. As they reached thirty miles an hour Rush reached in his shoulder holster and took out a thirty-eight revolver. He spun the cylinder once and looked out of the corner of his eye at Gay. Her eyes were on the gun in wide amazement.

"Have I given you the idea that you need protection from me?" she asked.

"No, I always figured my innocence was armor enough," said Rush.

He rolled down the window beside him and with the gun in his left hand reached out of the window and fired at the car ahead.

"Are you crazy?" asked Gay and for the first time she was shaken out of her customary poise. Her voice rose an octave. "Rush! That's Robin in the car ahead. He's your friend, remember?"

Rush emptied the gun at the car ahead and answering flashes came as Robin shot back. The night was torn into screaming fragments with the sound of the guns. Rush drew in his hand and tossed the gun to Gay. From his pocket he took a box and handed it to her.

"Fill it again," he said. "You can't have a gun battle without ammunition. Go on," he said as Gay stared at him, "fill it."

Slowly Gay's fingers opened the box. She pried at a shell with a fingernail. It came lose and fell in her palm. She looked at it a long second then smiled against her will. Her fingers went busily to work filling the gun.

"Here you are, you rat," she said. "I should have known you weren't man enough to shoot a sure enough bullet. Blanks are about your speed."

By this time Robin was firing again and Rush emptied the gun out of the window in his direction.

"This," said Rush, "is what is known as an object lesson. We're proving to the citizens of Forest City that the place is going to hell. We're giving them a gun battle right in their laps. I'm going to wake up this joint if it takes dynamite."

Robin and Rush continued to give the citizens a gun battle for just over twenty minutes, then in the silence while Gay reloaded his gun Rush heard the distant howl of a squad car. He gave two loud blasts on the horn and waved as Robin looked over his shoulder. Five minutes later they were a mile away and a mile from each other. Rush drove sedately to the door of Gay's apartment house and opened the door. He followed her up the walk, through the hall and to the door of her apartment.

"Do you suppose," he said at the door, "that I could steal an hour's sleep on your davenport?" He lowered his eyes demurely as if embarrassed by the words.

"My mother told me this would happen some day," said Gay. "I wish she'd told me what to do."

"I'm sure your mother would approve. My intentions are so honorable they hurt. I need an hour or so's sleep and I don't want to come in to the hotel at this time in the morning. Too many people would wonder where I'd been."

Gay tapped her toe on the wood floor.

"You'd rather they thought you'd been here all night," she said.

"Say, they will, won't they. That's fine. You can report that to Carney, too. He'll think you're really working at your new job."

"Go to hell," said Gay. "Come on in and get your sleep."

Fifteen minutes later Rush minus shoes, coat and shirt was stretched on Gay's davenport. She came out of the bedroom in a long white and very flowing negligee. Her red hair flamed over her shoulders and cascaded in a thousand waves against the white silk. She pirouetted once and stood before him.

"I hope you like this negligee. I brought it for exactly this kind of a situation. I'm damned if I thought it would be like this though."

She came to the davenport and sat on its edge. She leaned forward and kissed Rush full on the lips. Her hair fell forward and made a curtain on either side of her face and she and Rush were in a tiny space in time alone. It was a space lit with the glow of a lamp sifting through her hair.

Then she stood up and looked down at him. She looked down at him for a long time.

"Damn you," she said at last, "if I fall in love with you, you'll regret it till the day you die."

She turned and walked back into her bedroom closing the door after her.

The smell of coffee and the sound of bacon frying wakened Rush. He stretched muscles back into their original shape, swung his feet off the davenport on to the floor, scratched his head and ran his hand over sleepy eyes and down across a stubby chin. He stood up and walked to the door of the kitchen. Gay, dressed briefly in a halter and shorts looked up from a frying pan full of bacon.

"It's through the door to your right and across the bedroom," she said. "There's a razor on the top shelf of the cabinet."

Twenty minutes later, shaven, washed, and combed Rush knotted his tie and sat down across from Gay in the breakfast nook. He poured a cup of coffee and drank it black and hot before he spoke.

"Where's the morning paper?" he asked.

"Don't be so damn domestic," said Gay. "Last night was bad enough without you acting like a bored husband this morning."

Rush got up, walked around the end of the table, kissed her thoroughly and returned to his seat.

"Have you seen the morning paper, dear?" he asked.

"That's more like it. Not quite, but almost," said Gay.

She reached a hand down to the bench beside her and tossed the paper across the table. Rush spread it and poured a cup of coffee as he read the headlines. They were almost hysterical.

FOREST CITY IN GRIP OF CRIME WAVE

That was the banner. Column leads spoke of the posters and of a running gunbattle through the streets at an early morning hour. The police were mystified. Rush read them all thoroughly including one he hadn't expected. When he was through he folded the paper, turned it around and laid it in front of Gay, his finger pointing at a subhead.

"You saved my life," he said accusingly.

"It was nothing that any girl scout couldn't do," said Gay. "How did I do it?"

"You let me stay the night with you. Look." His finger stabbed at the column he had indicated. The head read—

BOMB BLAST IN HOTEL ROOM

The room, Gay noted, was 715. She raised eyebrows at Rush.

"I call that home. A modest place, but mine own."

All joking was gone from Gay.

"This has stopped being funny," she said. "They're playing for keeps."

"Do you think I'm playing for fun?" asked Rush. "I asked for it and I got it, only I wasn't there on time to receive it personally. I even expected it. But, my dear," he looked seriously across the table at Gay, "I've got some very lovely things in store for them, too. And they'll get them personally. They're on their last legs. When the mob that runs this town begins to go in for actual violence, they're on the way out."

Gay lit a cigarette and puffed angrily.

"You're so damn sure of yourself," she said.

"You think you're so damn invulnerable and all it will take is one bullet on a dark street and you're through. There's no more you. Where bullets are concerned you're like Achilles, only you're all heel."

Rush grinned.

"I hope I get what you mean," he said. "And let me point out the only error in your charge. I don't think I'm invulnerable. I've been shot at and shot often enough to know how much it hurts and how easy I am to get at if I'm not careful. Q.E.D. I'm always careful. Very careful."

He stood up from the table then and shrugged into his coat.

"Thanks for your hospitality and I'll see you this evening. I'll call about six and we'll eat somewhere."

"And spend the rest of the evening taking a long walk down dark alleys where no one can see us."

"You're inexperienced. We'll be much safer among the bright lights. People almost never shoot you there."

He kissed her solidly and left.

A cruising cab picked him up a block away and deposited him at the offices of the Forest City *Chronicle*. He found Bill Prime and Pedrick in Prime's office. Pedrick raised an eyebrow at him from a chair across the room.

"Among a lot of guys who have been lucky in love, you are the luckiest I've ever known. I hope you thanked that redhead for saving your life."

"I did," said Rush. "I did indeed."

"What the hell is this deal?" asked Prime.

"What deal?" asked Rush.

"Start with the bomb."

"That's one that missed me in more ways than one. I don't know who put it there, but I'd hate to think I couldn't get it in three guesses."

Prime nodded.

"Yeah. You're setting new records for personal unpopularity in certain quarters. But how about the gun battle?"

"Now, that's something else again," said Rush. "That is a grade A sample of my own brand of dynamite. I think I bought about ten thousand votes for Covington for the price of four boxes of blank cartridges and a half hour of my time."

Prime leaned across the desk and stared at him.

"You staged that with blanks?" he asked.

Rush nodded.

Price swore briefly under his breath.

"A phony," he said, "a goddam phony."

Rush narrowed eyes at him across the desk.

"I hope I can depend on you to keep it on the front page. I'd hate to have all this blow up in my face. I'd hate to do it but I'd throw you and your paper to the wolves in a minute if I thought you were backing out. Somebody hired me to come in here and it could have been you. I could think so and tell people that anyway."

"Put away your knife, Rush," said Pedrick. "Nobody's double-crossing you. It's you that the printer's ink in Bill's veins boils at the idea that he got taken in by a phony."

Prime swore again and then relaxed, his face loosening into a grin.

"Yes, goddamnit. I never thought I'd bite on a deal like that. But it was a good one and it ought to get you at least ten thousand votes." He chewed briefly on a fresh cigar, put a match to it and looked at Rush. "What next?" he asked.

"More dynamite," said Rush. "I don't know exactly what kind but I've got to keep things blowing up or the story'll get cold by Tuesday."

"Don't worry about that," said Prime. "That's only four days away. I'll feed them gang war and crime wave till they're full up to here." His palm sliced across his throat.

"Fair enough," said Rush. "I think I'll keep plugging though. I've got a couple of cracks I want to blast open before I'm through."

"Just be sure you keep out of the line of fire," said Pedrick. "Next time you may be sleeping at home."

"Heaven forbid," said Rush. "Now, I think I'll see if I have any clothes left and have lunch. See you later."

He left and headed for the hotel.

Chapter 14

A harried hotel manager showed Rush to his room. It was a shambles. However, Rush's luck held. The blast had centered under the bed and his clothes in the closet were untouched. There was a good deal of dust and dirt showered on his shirts and linen in the dresser but a laundry would fix them good as new. The only real damage from Rush's standpoint was done to a bottle of rye. It had shattered and run over the desk.

He calmed the hotel manager by promising not to sue the hotel. When promised a new room he followed him down the hall. He went into the coffee shop and spread a noon edition of the *Chronicle* across the table while waiting for his order to come. Bill Prime had been as good as his promise. He played the various stories for all they were worth. They read like a Hearst sheet in full cry. As he read, Rush wondered what ammunition he could dig up to throw on the fire. He didn't wonder long, nor did he have to dig for ammunition. The waitress stood over him with a plate suspended waiting for him to move the paper. Simultaneously as he moved a shot rang out just outside the coffee shop —the girl dropped the plate and Rush jumped as though the shot had hit him. The paper saved his clothes and he scrambled out of the booth and dodged around tables to the street door of the coffee shop. To his left, a matter of ten feet, a crowd of people were clustered around a huddled figure on the sidewalk. Rush shouldered his way in and looked down. There was something familiar about the lean tailored length huddled around a puddle of blood on the sidewalk. He almost got it in the slick hair, mustache and sideburns but not quite. He turned to the man beside him.

"Who is it?" he asked.

His neighbor didn't even look up.

"Joe Natale," he said. "Carney's right bower."

That was all Rush needed. He had seen the man in Carlo's the night of the great smell. He turned on his heel and elbowed his way out of the growing crowd. At its fringe he turned to go into the coffee shop when a hand fell on his shoulder.

"Mr. Henry?" said a voice like a saw in a pine knot.

He turned to face a shapeless man in rumpled clothes. Filmy eyes stared at him over pasty gray bags.

"What's on your mind?" asked Rush shaking off the hand.

"Hacker wants to see you at headquarters," said the voice.

"How'd he know I was here?"

"Saw you." The man flipped a thumb over his

shoulder. Rush followed it with his eyes and saw the Chief of Police sitting in a squad car directing the operations of his men. He left the shapeless man abruptly and walked over to Hacker.

"You want to see me?" he asked.

The chief looked out of the car window.

"Yeah," he said. "At headquarters. Get in."

"You're seeing me now," said Rush. "I'm eating."

"I'll see you at headquarters. Get in."

Rush looked at him for a moment then dropped his cigarette to the sidewalk and ground it out with his toe.

"I'm eating, Hacker," he said and turned away.

"Get him," said Hacker in a tired voice.

A pair of hands attached themselves to each of Rush's arms and he felt himself being forcibly moved back to the car. It was neatly done. Several pairs of eyes stared incuriously and turned back to the stretcher now being shoved into an ambulance. The car door opened and Rush was shoved into the back seat. Hacker issued orders to men through the door of the car, then waved the driver. The car shot away from the curb and headed for the police station.

Rush sat quietly during the trip to the station and the brief walk to the Chief's office. In the office Hacker walked behind his desk and motioned Rush to a chair. Two men in plain clothes came into the office and took chairs behind Rush. A uniform cop came in to stand behind Hacker. Hacker took his time about lighting a cigar. When he was satisfied with the light he looked at Rush through the cloud of smoke.

"You went too far, Henry!" he said.

Rush looked at him.

"You been getting away with murder this last week but now you went too far. We got you cold."

Rush looked at him unbelievingly.

"Are you going to pin this on me?" he asked.

Hacker nodded with satisfaction.

"It's cold," he said.

"Well, I'll be a name of a name," said Rush. "You big dumb hunk of lard. I've got an alibi as solid as your head. You couldn't hook me if you had an eye witness."

Hacker leaned across the desk.

"What kind of an alibi?" he asked softly.

"A cinch," said Rush. "I was—" he stopped dead. "Why, I believe you would," he said.

"Would what?" asked Hacker.

"Take care of my alibi. Book me, you big slob and I'll bring in my alibi. Until then you can sweat."

Hacker leaned back in his chair and surveyed the ceiling.

"Okay," he said in the general direction of the roof, "you got an alibi. At least we'll assume you got one for the moment. I got another charge for you. Conspiracy." He came forward in the chair and swung to face Rush. "If you ain't been doing these killings, you know who has. You hired them."

Rush laughed at him. Laughed loud.

"You know," said Hacker, "I wouldn't be surprised if you'd confess to something like that. And it'd sure be a load off my mind if you did." He nodded to the two plainclothesmen. "Why don't you boys arrange to take down Mr. Henry's confession." He shoved a sheet of paper across the desk. "It should be something along the lines I've indicated here on this paper. I'll be waiting for you." He grinned evilly at Rush.

The room was ten by ten with whitewashed walls and a bare cement floor sloping to a drain in one corner. There was a straight chair in the center of the room and a shaded light hanging from a cord to the ceiling. There were straps attached to the back of the chair. Two of them. One for each arm. They tied Rush in the chair and went to work.

It was simple at first. Open palm slaps from meaty hands. A tap or two from a night stick on the skin. Rush laughed. It got tougher then. Little tricks with cigarette coals. A thorough workout with a leaded hose. Full fisted blows in the face. Rush's grin was crooked but it was still a grin. Then they brought out a hammer and a heavy piece of iron. They had his fingers on the iron and the hammer raised when somebody pounded on the door. It was unlocked and a face peered into the room.

"Fix him up quick and get him up to Hacker's office."

There was a brief argument, briefer but violent cursing and Rush was unstrapped from the chair. They half led, half carried him to a lavatory where cold towels and more cold water revived him and reduced some of the swelling. He was on his own feet and maneuvering under his own power when he entered Hacker's office for the second time. Hacker was seated at his desk as though he might never have moved, but there was a difference. Hacker was a different man. He figuratively bowed and scraped in his effort to treat the whole affair as a joke, or at the most as an understandable error in judgment. He also writhed in spiritual agony. The reason for his abrupt reversal sat easily in a chair across the room.

"Take it easy, Hacker," said Matt Pedrick. "Mr. Henry knows you have the intelligence of a bright four year old. You don't have to prove it. Did the boys get rough, Rush?"

"They were about to. Consider me in your debt."

"Think nothing of it and let me apologize for our Chief of Police. He got the job because he could count to twenty without taking off his shoes. Police work remains a mystery to him."

"Now, Mr. Pedrick—" started Hacker.

"I think it smells a little in here, Rush. Shall we go?"

"It stinks," said Rush. "Let's."

On the sidewalk, Rush refused Pedrick's offer of a ride.

"I've still got the rented car somewhere around here and I've a quick trip I have to make. I think the time has come for me to have further words with Mr. Covington."

Rush found Covington at his home. He waited while he finished lunch and then walked with him into the garden. There, surrounded by a high hedge, they sat in comfortable lawn furniture and talked. That is, Covington talked. His tone was a nice blend of sorrow and anger.

"I'm taking the lightest possible view of the things that have happened in the past week in Forest City, Henry, but even glossing over minor accidents such as the wrecked night club and the stink bombs in Max Carney's place things have come to such a state that I can no longer countenance them. There have been three murders and I personally heard a running gun battle in the streets. It has to stop."

"It will," said Rush. "It'll stop Tuesday evening when you're elected mayor. You'll stop it yourself."

"You can't contemplate more bloodshed."

"I didn't even contemplate the bloodshed you've

had. Beau Marr was shot after I had been in town a bare half dozen hours. I'd never even heard his name. The man who was shot this morning was a complete stranger to me."

Covington frowned.

"Do you mean to say that none of this was your doing? After the things you told me when you first came to my office."

"Let me tell you again what I'm doing," said Rush. "I'm doing everything I can to arouse suspicion among the men who have been running your town. They have had such a smooth running operation that it was impossible to convince the average man that anything was wrong. I'm convincing them. I've tried to set them at each others throats. I'll admit that that is probably why Sully got killed. But you can't clean up a city like this without breaking a few dishes. Sully was just a soiled old plate and he had it coming. Beyond that I'm stage managing a few effects that may not be quite what they seem. I had hoped that a little false sound and fury would be all that was necessary but somewhere along the line somebody else drew a hand. They play rougher than I do."

"Who could it be—not Carney surely."

"I hardly think so. Max is smart enough to know that blood on the street is just the kind of thing that'll ruin him. He also knew there was no reason for shooting anybody."

"Then who for heaven's sake and why?"

"When you give me that answer I'll have a lot of other answers for you."

"Well, answers or no answers it's got to stop. I could never face myself or my friends if I knew that I climbed to the mayor's office through a pile of dead bodies. I must ask you to stop your efforts immediately and leave Forest City."

"I'm afraid that's out of your hands, Mr. Covington," said Rush. "I'm going to elect you in spite of yourself and then I hope you'll be—"

Rush broke off in mid word. A twig of the hedge had moved a fraction of an inch and no breeze stirred its neighborhood branches. Then just above that twig a darker shape appeared and for a second sunlight glinted against the green of the hedge. Rush was out of his chair in a diving lunge for Covington. He caught the older man full in the chest and rolled over him tumbling chair and all to the ground. In the same second a sharp report rang out, an echo rapped back and a branch of the hedge behind the spot Covington had been seated fluttered to the ground. Rush roughly shoved Covington behind a tree, then in a crouching run, drawing a gun from his shoulder as he moved, he angled across the lawn to a corner of the hedge where a flagged path ran through a break.

He could have saved the steps. He lowered his

head to the ground and looked around a corner of the hedge but his quarry had gone. In the distance a motor throbbed into life and roared away. Slowly he regained his feet and walked back to Covington who was now standing erect brushing himself off.

"What was that?" he asked angrily.

Rush told him.

"You were slated to be number four," he said.

Covington stared at him digesting the unpleasant truth. As he stood there he seemed to grow in stature. His shoulders came back and his chin went up.

"I have been mistaken, Henry. You seem to know more about this thing than I do. Stay in Forest City. Elect me by any means you can. Then come around and tell me how to clean up my city. I'll listen to you then."

He turned and walked back into the house. Rush watched his retreating back with a small grin. Silently he thanked the unseen gunman. The mayor-to-be had almost been a problem—the gunman had solved it for him.

Rush found Gay sitting by her telephone literally waiting for him to call.

"I've been just languishing here waiting for you to call, big boy," she said.

"Big boy?" said Rush. "Is this Westlake 4191?"

"Of course it is, you silly one. Who did you think

it was?" Her voice was loaded with a false gaiety.

"Is this Gay Wimberly?" asked Rush.

"Of course. Who did you think it'd be—Lana Turner?"

"What in the hell has happened to you?" He had a sudden thought. "Are you drunk?" he asked.

"No, but it sounds like a good idea. Why don't you come up here? We'll have a party. Just us two. Isn't that cozy?"

Rush's brow furrowed and he looked at the receiver as if it were playing him tricks. Then he got it.

"Are you alone?" he asked.

"Of course not, silly."

"Are you trying to decoy me up there for somebody?"

"Oh, I'd love to."

"Carney?"

"Of course."

"Okay, Circe. Tell him you've made a deal. You've decoyed me. I'll be there in a half an hour."

"You're the sweetest boy," giggled Gay. "You be careful. I want you to get here in one piece."

"And leave the same way. Don't worry, I'll bring my G-Man detective badge. They'll leave me alone then."

Rush hung up then and immediately made another call. When he was through with that one he left the phone booth and walked through the lobby of the hotel to the bar.

Chapter 15

Rush pushed the button outside of Gay's apartment a punctual half hour later. She came to the door in person and looked up at him from under quizzically raised brows. He winked at her and put his arms around her and kissed her soundly. In her ear he whispered.

"Everything's okay. Don't worry."

Aloud, Gay said to him:

"The strangest thing, dear. Just after you called Mr. Carney dropped by. When he heard you were coming he insisted on waiting. He wanted to talk to you."

"Always glad to see an old friend," said Rush. He stepped around Gay and into the room. Carney was seated in the middle of the davenport, a drink in one hand and a cigar in the other. Seated strategically, in corners of the room were his two boys, Junior and his pal. "Hello, Maxie," said Rush. "Nice to see you again."

"Sit down, Henry," said Max Carney. His cigar pointed at a chair opposite the davenport.

"Sure, Maxie," said Rush. "How about a drink, Gay?"

Gay poured a drink and put it in his hand. He lit a cigarette and blew smoke at the ceiling.

"Well, what's on your mind, Carney?" he asked.

"I wanted to finish that talk we had."

"I thought it was finished. I thought when I told you to get out of town that there wasn't anything left to say."

"There is though. I got the same thing to say to you and I mean it."

"You mean you think I was joking?" asked Rush.

"You might as well have been. You aren't going to be able to do anything about it."

"You fascinate me, Carney. You're always so sure of yourself. How do you know I'm not going to be able to do anything about it?"

"Because I'm going to put you where you can't do anything at all."

Gay gasped behind Rush.

"Why, Maxie," said Rush. "That sounds very much as if you were thinking of having me knocked off. I warned you about that. It'd be the biggest mistake of your career. You'd think the roof fell in on you inside of twenty-four hours."

Carney smiled and his lips thinned to knife edges.

"It was nice of you to warn me about that, Henry. But I've got a way around that. I'm going to hang onto you till this is over then you can do anything you want to."

"Oh, but that would be the same as knocking me over. If the paper doesn't hear from me every twenty-four hours they get practically frantic."

"They'll hear from you all right. You'll call them. I'll make a point of seeing that you call them and—" he paused dramatically, "and tell them what I tell you to tell them."

"A brilliant scheme, Maxie," said Rush. "But what if I won't talk?"

"You'll talk all right." Carney let his eyes swing to his left and upward to Gay's face. "I think you'll talk, or sing, or stand on your head if I tell you to. All I'll have to do is turn Junior loose on your girl friend here and you'll turn over and play dead."

Rush smiled and it wasn't a pretty thing.

"You bastard," he said. "I think you'd really do that. I think you even think you could get away with it." He looked at the two uglies in the corners of the room. "Are these the troops you brought to take me in? Haven't they told you how I treat them? I wouldn't trust those two cretins to bring in Shirley Temple." He stopped and scowled in disgust. "Hell, this is silly. Let's get it over. Come on in, Smoky and Duffy."

The bedroom door opened behind Carney and Smoky and Duffy stepped into the room, guns in hand.

"Now, take your hired hands and get the hell out of here. Dammit, Carney. Can't you get it through your head that your methods went out with Al Capone? We've smartened up on our side of the street. Now blow and impress it on Junior and his pal there that if they get in my way again I'm going to beat the bloody bejesus out of them. I'm tired of stumbling over them everywhere I go, and that includes you. Go on, get out."

Carney nodded his head toward the door and without a word Junior and his friend walked out into the hall. Carney followed them in complete silence.

When the door had closed Rush turned to Gay.

"You were terrific," he said. "It would have been tough if I'd walked in here cold. I'd have had to mess up your apartment to get rid of those termites."

"I was scared," said Gay, "scared to death."

"It was nothing. Just be damn thankful you have a fire escape that opens on your bedroom window."

Another head popped into the room from the bedroom.

"Can I come in?" asked Robin Twist.

"I thought I told you to stay under cover," said Rush.

"I was just bringing up the rear. In case things got out of hand I was going to pop in and save you. I always wanted to be a hero."

Rush looked around the room.

"Well we're all here but Merwin so we might as well have a brief council. I wanted to see you guys anyway. Where is Merwin by the way?"

"I stuck Merwin in your hotel room. I wanted to be sure it was clean when you came in tonight," said Robin.

"I don't think I'm going to come in tonight," said Rush.

"If this is an improper suggestion you fellows are witnesses," said Gay. "He's got to follow through."

"No, I think I'd better get to Chicago by tomorrow morning."

They all looked at him.

"I thought you'd been in Chicago," said Gay.

"Something new, Rush?" asked Robin.

"Not exactly new," said Rush. "It's something that's been growing on me."

"I hope it looks nice on you," said Gay.

"I think I've had the same thought," said Robin. "You need Mr. X."

"I'm afraid I do."

"Isn't there something we can talk about that I understand?" asked Gay.

"It's an act," said Smoky. "They were spies together once and now they always talk in code. When they get started like this the only thing to do is pour a drink and sweat it out."

He poured three slugs of whiskey and handed one to Gay and one to Duffy.

"Okay, get going. We'll latch on when we begin to understand."

"It's really quite simple. Somebody has gone trigger happy in this town. There have been three murders and this afternoon somebody took a pot shot at Covington. The only one of the big three left is Carney and for all his antique ideas of how to be a gangster, he's no fool. He had too good a thing to risk losing it all just to be the only boss. He could have sat still for years and milked a million dollars clear out of this town. So it has to be somebody else."

"And that leaves Mr. X," said Robin.

"It does indeed," said Rush. "I have tried and tried but I can't figure anybody else with a big enough stake in this town to start knocking off the citizens. It's either X or some other unknown quantity who wants to take things over."

"Or maybe both," said Smoky.

Rush turned his head very slowly and looked at Smoky. He looked at him for a long time before he spoke.

"Take a bow, Smoky," he said at last. "I should have thought of that myself. It's a perfect angle. X hires me to come in and clean up the town. Then when it gets around what I'm trying to do, he knocks off the head men in the rackets and I get blamed for it. Then when I leave he takes over where Carney and Sully and Marr left off. Very pretty. A neat scheme. But it won't work. When I get through with this town the combined efforts of Al Capone, Legs Diamond and Lucky Luciano couldn't get it organized again. I think X miscalculated. I don't think he figured on the election. I've convinced Covington that I can show him how to run a clean town, and I can. I also am going to get Covington elected. After that X is out in the cold."

"But, in the meantime," said Robin.

"That's the rub, Robin," said Rush. "In the meantime he may take another shot at Covington and not miss. He might even get me. So I've got to get X first if I can. That's why I'm going to Chicago. The trail started there so I'll go there to pick it up."

An hour later Rush was in a charter plane bound for Chicago and five hours later he was in his office lavatory removing the stains of travel.

Chapter 16

Sharp at ten o'clock Rush was in the law offices of Leach, Carruthers and Leach. Five minutes later he was closeted with Aaron Leach. He laid his cards on the table. They were not pretty cards and Aaron Leach was visibly disturbed by them.

"I hope, Mr. Henry," he said, "that it is not in your mind that I am a party to any such conspiracy as you suggest."

"Not at all. I am sure the idea is as distasteful to you as it is to me. However, I am certain in my own mind that you have been used to further just such a conspiracy. A rather vicious thing is happening in Forest City and I want to stop it. I am convinced that the only way I can stop it is by reaching the man you represented in hiring me. I am quite willing to forfeit the ten thousand dollar fee but I must find that man and stop further and needless bloodshed."

"You need not worry about your fee, Mr. Henry," said Leach stiffly. "If you perform the task for which you were retained, my firm will make good the fee you were promised."

"It isn't that," said Rush. "It's gone beyond money. Till now the men who have been killed have earned it one way or the other. It was part of the way they lived. But now innocent people are in danger and I don't propose to let anything happen to them if I can possibly stop them."

"You realize, of course, that I don't know the name of the man for whom I secured your services. My only contact with him was through his lawyer."

"But you know the lawyer. Give me his name. Through him I can find X."

Leach considered the request for a long moment. Finally he shook his head.

"In view of the absolute secrecy that was requested by my correspondent in Forest City, I'm afraid it would be unethical for me to reveal his name on such strictly circumstantial evidence as you have presented. You might be wrong, Mr. Henry."

"Of course I might. I might be right too and an innocent man may be killed while you wrestle with your conscience over ethics. That, if you'll pardon the expression, is a hell of thing to have on your conscience."

"It is indeed, Mr. Henry. I pray you are wrong." The older man stood up as though to end the interview. "You are a detective, Mr. Henry, and by all reports a good one. You should be able to devise some means of learning my correspondent's name. After all. He learned mine."

The older man smiled and stepped around his desk to open the door for Rush. Rush was halfway out of the building before he got the hint in the old lawyer's last words. He turned instantly on his heel and went back to the outer office of Leach, Carruthers and Leach. There he found a faded spinster presiding over the combined switchboard and information desk.

"What was Mr. Aaron Leach's school?" he asked.

"He attended Harvard," she replied.

"And his class?"

"Mr. Leach graduated in 1906."

"Thank you," said Rush with feeling.

In the lobby of the building he found a phone booth and dialed the number of the *Express*. Seconds later Pappy Daley was on the phone.

"Rush here," he said.

"In Chicago?"

"Right."

"What are you doing here. Is the Forest City thing over?"

"Not till next Wednesday. Right now I need information and you can get it for me faster than anybody else."

"Shoot."

"I want a list of names of the graduating class of 1906 from the Harvard Law School and I want all of their present addresses."

"I'll put our New York bureau on it. They should be able to get it from the school in a couple of hours. What shall I do with it?"

"Shoot it to me airmail special registered at once. It's vital. Better yet. I'll call you sometime tonight. Take it with you and leave word where I can get you."

"Check. I should have it by six. What time is it now?"

Rush looked at his watch.

"It's eleven-thirty. I'll be in Forest City by four or four-thirty. I'll give you a call then on the chance that you'll have it. It's really important."

He hung up then and caught a taxi for the long ride to the airport. His watch showed exactly four o'clock as the wheels of the plane touched the runway in Forest City. The cab ride to the hotel took thirty minutes. At exactly four-thirty he got Pappy on the phone again.

"Got it, Rush. Harvard was glad to oblige the New York office of the Chicago *Express*."

"Give," said Rush.

"Do you want them all, or do you just want the one from Forest City?"

"Give me the one from Forest City, mindreader. I'm in a hurry."

"A gentleman by the name of King S. Wellwood graduated in 1906 and at last report to the alumni committe was in practice in Forest City. Is that what you want?"

"That's it. Thanks, Pappy."

"Always a pleasure." His voice became serious.

"I'm getting some pretty mean stuff on the press wires from Forest City. Is it getting hot?"

"It's ready to boil."

"Well, tell Smoky he's still working for me. I'll expect a story."

"You'll get it. I'll make a point of sending it myself."

"Will it be like the blow-off in Weston?"

"I doubt it. This is a different deal. It may not be much of a news story when it breaks, unless you consider a multiple murder in Forest City important."

"Who got killed?"

"That's just it. Chicago never heard of these guys but they were pretty important here."

"Well, shoot me what you get as soon as it breaks."

"Will do. So long, Pappy."

Rush walked to the dressing table and poured a drink from a bottle of rye that someone had placed there. Merwin, he supposed. Then he walked to the closet to check through his clothes. He was half in the closet peering at the hangers when a voice shattered the stillness of the room.

"Okay, I see you. Put em up—high!"

Rush turned slowly, disgust heavy on his face.

"Put the gun away, Merwin. It's only me."

Merwin stepped into the room closing the door behind him.

"Gosh, boss. I'm sorry. I thought you was in Chicago and Twist, he told me to keep this place clean. I didn't know it was you."

"It's okay, Merwin." He poured another drink and looked thoughtfully through it at the fading daylight filtering through the window. Then he went to the phone and called Matt Pedrick.

"I want to hire me a lawyer, Matt. I want some legal information."

"Will the attorney for the paper do?"

"No, I want a brand new lawyer, just out of law school."

"A fledgling?" Pedrick's voice mirrored his curiosity.

"Yes, it's a rather odd thing I want and ingenuousness is a requisite. He can't seem too erudite."

"Try a young fellow named Curran. You'll find him in the book. His office is in the Merchant's Building. He's as new as they come."

"Thanks, Matt. I'll tell you about it later. I want to get onto him."

Ten minutes later Rush caught young Mr. Curran locking his door and found little difficulty in persuading him to reopen his office. The interior looked as though he could stand a paying client or two. Rush put his business before him with only a few sentences of explanation.

"It's very important to me and to the good health of several other people to know the names of everybody who keep King S. Wellwood on an annual retainer."

Rush felt that X, if he were a client of Wellwood's would be a permanent one and that X would never trust a lawyer with whom he had had no previous dealings. Curran was doubtful.

"I hardly think that would be ethical."

"To hell with ethics. I argued ethics with another member of your profession all morning. I want facts. Human lives are involved and the easier and quieter I get this information the better chance I have to save them."

"Can't you tell me a little more?"

"No," said Rush bluntly. "There's a hundred dollar bill waiting for the answer to my question." A little more kindly he said. "If it will ease your conscience any please take my word for it that it is desperately important that I get the information I want. Also that it will be used only as a lead to other information. Also, it will never be known that you gave me the information."

Rush couldn't decide which of his arguments won. But he won.

"All right," said Curran reluctantly. "I can give you a fairly complete list right away. I was something of a protege of his and until I graduated I worked summers in his office preparing papers and that kind of thing."

"How soon is right away?"

"Say an hour."

"I'll be in my room at the hotel. Bring it there and I'll give you the hundred dollars."

Curran was punctual. Almost exactly an hour later he knocked on the door of Rush's room. Inside he tossed a paper across the bed to him.

"That's just about it. I checked through the classified directory to refresh my memory and that is pretty complete. There may be a few small clients I've missed but all the big ones and the estates he handles are there."

Without looking at the list Rush took a hundred dollars from a wad of paper money on the dressing table and tossed it to Curran.

"Thanks, Curran, and if you begin to lose sleep about this just remember that you may have saved a life or two including mine. Come around in a week and I'll explain it to you. You'll feel better then."

Curran left, the bill still clenched tightly in his fist. Rush picked up the list and began to read. It was a long list. Mr. King S. Wellwood had a profitable clientele. It seemed a respectable one, too. So respectable that Rush didn't recognize a name on it. A few were familiar, their names being part of well known firm names in the city, but not a one had even touched the fringes of his path through Forest City. He sighed and tossed the paper away. It was a hundred dollars kicked away. It only told him that he had further digging to do.

Rush remembered that Pedrick had mentioned a party at his apartment that evening. He reached for the phone and again called Pedrick. This time at the apartment.

"What time is your party set to blow, Matt?" he asked.

"Why, I expect the small fry and hard drinkers to turn up about eight. The bigger shots and those who can afford their own liquor will start coming about ten."

"Who'll be there?"

"The people I laughingly call my spies. My sources in other words. I throw one of these every so often for everybody who ever gave me a tip on a story. I thought you'd enjoy it. It gets quite raucous before it's through."

"I'll enjoy it all right." He paused for a moment. "Matt, would it be inconvenient if Gay and I got there a little early, say seven o'clock. I'm at a dead end for some information and you're about the only one who can give it to me."

"You'll be welcome, both to come and to dig anything I'm carrying in this garbage can I call my mind. I'll have a drink ready for your out-stretched hand."

"Thanks, Matt."

Rush hung up. He hoped without much optimism that Pedrick would be able to tell him what he wanted. If that failed he might have to go up against Wellwood himself and that in itself might be fatal. He shrugged his shoulders and once more reached for the phone. This time the number he gave was the one for the phone in Gay's apartment.

Chapter 17

Pedrick was as good as his word. He answered Rush's ring with a glass in each hand. He handed one to Gay and one to Rush.

"Come in," he said. "Take the best chairs and be comfortable. When the mob gets here you'll be on your feet for an hour or two and the air will be thick enough to float the Queen Mary. Be comfortable while you can."

Rush and Gay sat on a low divan and Pedrick sat astraddle a straight back chair his arms folded on its back, a drink in his hand.

"Well, what do I know that you want to know?" he asked.

"This is pretty confidential, Matt, so I won't tell you why I want to know. You'll learn soon enough. I just want to know everything there is to know about a lawyer named King Wellwood."

"Wellwood?" asked Pedrick. "What on earth has King got to do with anything you're interested in?"

"That's just it, Matt. I can't tell you right now. I want some background on him."

"That's easy enough. Harvard Law in the early 1900's, back to practice in his father's firm. His father died in the twenties and he took in a young partner, a guy named Bell. He's kind of a drone—

does most of the work, I'm told, while King does the court work and keeps up the front. Very successful. Married. No children. Big house in Country Club Place." He took a swallow of his drink and looked at Rush. "Enough?"

"No," said Rush. "That's not quite the sort of thing I want. How are his ethics? Is he greedy for anything? Does he have any complexes?"

"King? Hell, I don't know. He's an acquaintance. I meet him here and there and he always calls me Matt and I call him King but we're not personal friends. I can tell you this. He's never hit my column and if there were a screw loose there anywhere he'd have made it one way or the other. I don't even have a file on him and that means he keeps it pretty clean."

"How's his bank account?"

"I don't know but I can find out." He went to the phone and dialed a number. He talked for a moment in a low voice then hung up and came back to straddle his chair. "Excellent. No exact figures, but King S. Wellwood will never go hungry, not if he stops taking money for his work beginning tomorrow. He is in the bucks."

Rush drained his drink and puffed thoughtfully on his cigarette. There was little more he could ask without giving away his reason for questioning and he didn't want to do that just yet. He closed the subject.

"Okay, Matt. I may be mistaken. Let it slide for now. I'll explain after I'm sure."

Matt shrugged his shoulders philosophically. At that moment a ring on the doorbell brought him to his feet and he opened the door to admit Kit English. Her arms were loaded with packages which she deposited on a table in the kitchen.

"I don't know why I go to this trouble. This mob of thugs won't know what they're shoving in their mouths. They'd be happy with pig knuckles and sauerkraut but you have to give them caviar." She looked up at Gay. "Come on, Wimberly, put on an apron, you're going to work."

The girls busied themselves making canapes and Rush and Matt went into the large living room. Matt looked quizzically over his newly filled glass at Rush. His mouth was open to ask a question when someone leaned on the bell with a heavy hand and gave it a loud shave and a haircut beep beep.

"Lord," said Pedrick. "They're starting early tonight. Get behind the bar, man. You've got to earn your booze tonight."

He went to the door and swung it open. From the open hallway Rush could hear mixed voices shouting hellos and Pedrick's lighter voice mingling with a greeting. From that time on he was busy mixing drinks. The doorbell was never still and the bar was never free of an outstretched hand waiting to be filled with a drink. He lost track of the time and was astonished when he looked at his wrist watch to realize it was twelve o'clock. He looked over the sea of heads and saw Gay passing a tray of hors d'oeuvres. Kit came to stand at his elbow.

"Has Matt left you here alone all evening?"

Rush admitted that that was the case.

"I'll fix that. Matt!" she called. Matt came elbowing his way through the crowd. "Get yourself behind this bar and work awhile. Rush has hardly had time to pour himself a drink."

Rush knew better but he gladly accepted the hefty slug she poured him and let her lead him away as Matt took over at the bar.

"Come on," she said. "Get a breath of fresh air. That stuff in there has been breathed thirty times all ready." She led him through double glass doors to a small balcony projecting above the inner court of the apartment building. She closed the doors behind them and breathed deeply of the night air.

"That's better," she said. "Although I'm surprised that nobody else has discovered this spot. Last time Matt threw one of these parties he caught two couples in what amounted to flagrante delecto at one and the same time out here. One at each end of the balcony."

"That's pleasant," said Rush. "I imagine it was uncomfortable, though."

Kit took a cigarette from the package Rush offered, lit it, dragged savagely blowing the smoke out of both nose and mouth. She looked up at Rush and shrugged her shoulders. Then she let out her breath with a long sigh.

"I think I ought to tell you I brought you out here for a reason," she said.

"You flatter me," said Rush. "But what if Matt comes out again?"

"I don't see—oh, the flagrante delecto. No, I choose my spots better than that. No, I wanted to ask a favor."

"Again, you flatter me. What can I do for you?"

"I want to talk to you in private and just as soon as possible. It's very important."

"This is quite private," suggested Rush.

"No, somebody might come out here any minute. It has to be absolutely private."

"What would you suggest?" asked Rush.

"Could I possibly come to your room to-night?"

"The gallant thing for me to say would be that you could come to my room any night. But I don't think that's what you want." Rush considered. "Yes, you can go up there and wait for me if you wish. It may be some time. I'll give you my key and you can wait if you want to."

"Oh, thank you." She breathed another deep sigh. "That's a relief. I was afraid you'd put me off and it is so desperately important that I see you tonight."

Rush looked at his watch. It was nearly one o'clock.

"What time does this mob clear out?"

"Oh, they'll be there for hours yet."

"Well, I think I'll take Gay home now. That'll shorten your wait and make it easier all around."

"I'll probably leave before the party's over. It usually gets pretty rough about this time. I'm not really fastidious but some of these people turn my stomach. I always say orgies are such personal things, don't you think? A crowd spoils a good one."

Rush had no answer to that. He opened the door to the living room and they stepped back into the heat and smoke and noise. He found Gay in the kitchen and put his arms around her untying her apron as he pulled her toward him. He kissed her briefly on the lips and turned her toward the door.

"We are blowing this fly trap," he said. "I've had a big day and I need sleep."

Rush made his need for rest stand up as an excuse and with a last drink and an almost brotherly kiss he left Gay's apartment. His watch gave him two-ten as he walked down the sidewalk toward his parked car. Fifteen minutes later he was outside the door of his room in the hotel. Having given his key to Kit he tried the door with his hand. The knob turned and the door swung away from him into the room. The light was on. He pushed the door away from him and stood just outside the door looking in. As the door swung open it revealed Kit lying on his bed holding a drink in one hand and a cigarette in the other.

"Welcome," she said. "Come into my parlor."

"You're no spider, and I'm no fly. As a matter of fact this is no parlor. But I'll come in."

He closed the door behind him and walked to the dressing table to pour himself a drink. He swallowed deeply and turned to the bed. He looked at Kit stretched on the spread. She made a pretty picture with her blonde hair spread in what must have been calculated folds on the pillow. He walked to the edge of the bed and sat down. He took the cigarette from her fingers and dragged on it.

"Well, what gives? I'm pretty sure it's not my manly figure that has dragged you up here."

"Don't be too sure," she said.

"Thank you," said Rush.

Kit sat up in the bed and put a hand on Rush's as it lay on the spread.

"No, it wasn't your manly figure although it certainly has its points. I came up here to offer you fifteen thousand dollars to get out of town."

"Where did you ever get hold of fifteen thousand dollars and why do you want me out of town?" asked Rush.

"It isn't my fifteen thousand dollars," she said. She shut her eyes and squeezed the lids tightly together for a moment. "Oh, I'm doing this all wrong. I'm so mixed up I don't know what to do."

Rush looked at her thoughtfully.

"Look," he said finally. "You don't need to figure out an act to put on. Just tell me what happened. I'll figure it out for myself."

Kit opened her eyes and looked at him.

"Maybe that'd be best. This evening before I started for Matt's I got a phone call. It was a man with a kind of muffled voice. He said he wanted me to run an errand for him. I was going to hang up when he said there was five thousand dollars in it for me if I did it right. I listened then—"

She broke off then and looked down at her hand on Rush's.

"I don't suppose I can explain what five thousand dollars would mean to me. I could get away from this town. I could travel a little. I could find a place I liked and live there. I hate this town!" Her voice rose and fell in what was almost a sob.

"What about Matt?" asked Rush.

"Oh, Matt's all right. I like him very much. But he has too much fun here. He'd never leave Forest City. But then Forest City has always been nice to him. I was born on the wrong side of the tracks. I can never go to all the homes Matt does. He could never marry me without losing his friends out in Country Club Place. I'd hate that, too, just like I hate the town. My dad drove a garbage wagon in the bottoms when I was a kid. Nobody'd ever forget that. I want to get away. Sometimes at night I wake up in a cold sweat and I've been dreaming about meeting some of Matt's society friends and hearing them ask who my father was."

Rush got up and poured them both a drink.

"Okay. Now I know why you want five grand. How were you supposed to earn it?"

"By getting you to leave town. I was to offer you fifteen thousand. Then if you accepted I'd get twenty thousand through the mail tomorrow and I was to keep five thousand."

"And if I refuse?"

Kit hesitated.

"I can answer that, I think," said Rush. "If I refused you were to tell me that I wouldn't last twenty-four hours. That I'd be taken care of for good."

Kit nodded, her eyes lowered, looking down at nothing.

"I think you'd better tell them I refuse," said Rush.

Kit's head jerked up. Her eyes were wide staring into his.

"Oh, but you can't."

"I'm afraid I can," said Rush.

He stood up and walked to the window. Kit was off the bed in a flash of silken limbs. She came to stand directly in front of him before the window.

She moved very close and her hands rested on his hips.

"Look at me, Rush," she said and her voice was husky with emotion. Rush looked directly into her eyes. "I'll up the offer," she said. "I'll go with it. You can have me for as long as you like, only leave town. I'll go wherever you go and stay as long as you like." Her lips parted and her breath came quicker. "Don't think it will be hard to take. Your manly figure does have its points."

Her hands on his hips moved around him and pulled him to her. Her parted lips came up to meet his and her body flowed forward the inches that had seperated them. Under his lips hers moved slowly and her body trembled against his then strained to him.

An unfamiliar pulse throbbed in Rush's temple —his hands tightened on her shoulders, and he took one stumbling step with her away from the window then slowly he relaxed his hold on her shoulders, slower still his hands dropped behind his back and grasped hers. He pulled her arms from around his back and stepped away from her.

"No, Kit," he said. "No. It won't go down. I can't swallow it."

She looked up at him through eyes in which tears brimmed to overflowing.

"You mean you don't believe me?"

"It doesn't matter whether I believe you or not.

I don't know what I believe. It's my pride that won't go down. I can't swallow it no matter how hard I try. I'm afraid you'll have to hunt your five grand somewhere else."

Kit stared at him unbelievingly for a long moment. Then turned blindly and stumbled to the bed falling on her face on the cover. Her shoulders shook in spasms of sobbing that was almost unbearable because it was totally silent.

Rush poured a drink and slugged it down straight. He poured another and lit a cigarette. He sat in the chair and waited. Minutes passed and the figure on the bed became still. Then abruptly she sat up, got to her feet and walked to the dressing table. She drank deeply from the neck of the bottle. She opened her purse and did feminine things to her face. Then she picked up her purse and turned around to face Rush. In her face was acceptance. Her eyes looked at him with no trace of rancor, rather with something that almost approached sadness.

"Well," she said. "I tried. It was a good try, too."

"Yes, Kit," said Rush, "it was a good try."

She walked to the door, opened it, and closed it behind her without a word.

Chapter 18

Rush was up at eight-thirty and hurried through breakfast in the coffee shop to make the nine-thirty meeting he had scheduled in his room. It was time for action. Things had been quiet for better than twenty-four hours. It was time to remind the public once more that things were not as they seemed in Forest City and that Tuesday was the time to change them at the polls. He contemplated various forms of dynamite as the elevator climbed toward his floor.

As he had expected his little group was in his room ahead of him. Smoky had picked the lock as usual. Knowing that Smoky would rather pick a lock than use a key, Rush was no longer surprised at finding the mammoth reporter on the other side of any door.

Rush stood in the door and surveyed his army. They were all there. Smoky stretched full length on the bed, Robin at the window, Merwin sitting on the edge of the bed studying a scratch sheet, his lips moving as he read. Duffy sat in the arm chair his short legs bent over one arm.

"Hy, Rush," said Duffy. "Come in."

"Thanks, Duff," said Rush.

"Nice bed you got here," called Smoky from

his supine position. "A hell of a lot better than that plank I have to sleep on every night." He wriggled to his side and propped his head on his hand. "Got any booze? I'm a man who likes a drink in the morning."

"Right· on the dresser. I'm surprised there's any left. Pour your own."

"You're closest, Duff, pour me a large hooker."

Duffy swung his feet to the floor and walked to the dresser. He uncorked the bottle of rye and poured a half inch in a glass.

"I got a bad taste myself. This ought to fix it." He poured the ounce of whiskey down his throat and shook his head. "Rotgut," he said. He put the glass down and reached for the bottle. His hand hovered for a moment over the bottle, wavered, then flew to his collar. A gurgling sound grew deep in his throat. His knees buckled and he fell across the dresser. He retched twice and vomited on the dresser top. Then slowly almost deliberately his body tilted a little to the right and faded to the floor.

Rush was at his side kneeling over him before he hit the floor. His hand went inside Duffy's shirt over his heart. He held it there for a long time. Then he stood up very slowly and looked around the room. Every eye was on him. He shook his head slowly.

"Not a sign of heartbeat," he said. "It must have

been cyanide." He looked down at Duffy. "Thanks, Duff," he said. "It should have been me. If I hadn't overslept, it would have been me. Nine mornings out of ten I take a slug of whiskey instead of a mouth wash. This morning I was late so I missed. So Duffy gets it."

Robin walked over to the dresser and examined the bottle carefully. He smelled it, poured a little in a glass and looked through it at the light.

"The bottle's half empty, Rush. How'd the stuff get in it?"

Rush shook his head.

"That's what bothers me, Robin. I was drinking out of it last night just before I went to bed. When did you get in here?"

Robin looked at Smoky.

"It was about nine-fifteen, wasn't it?"

Smoky nodded.

"Maybe nine-twenty," he said.

"Then there was nobody in the room for three quarters of an hour. You aren't the only guy who can pick locks, Smoky. Also, there're always more keys to hotel rooms." He walked to the phone.

"What're you gonna do, Rush?" asked Smoky.

"Call the cops. We can't hide this one."

He put in a call to police headquarters and asked homicide to send a squad. Then he hung up and turned back to his gang.

"I want you all to scram, one at a time. Get out

before the cops come. Go down a floor or up a floor before you take the elevator and don't know each other on the way out."

"But, Rush—" Smoky started to protest.

"No, Smoky. You'll do me more good on the outside. The cops'll try to hang this one on me and they may make it stick. If you were here they'd toss you in too. I need somebody outside to get some work done on my side. They'll just pick up that bottle, lift my prints and railroad me. I'll need help. The stuff was put there for me. It got Duffy, but it's liable to get me too if I don't get a break. That's your job. Get me a break."

They didn't like it but they recognized the logic of Rush's argument. They slipped out of the room leaving Rush with Duffy. Ten minutes later a hammering on the door announced the law. They ran absolutely true to Rush's predictions. They asked a question or two. Looked at the bottle, at Duffy then at Rush. Inside of five minutes they had handcuffs on Rush and he was out of the room and on his way to a cell.

It was different this time. No meeting with the Chief of Police, no visit to the whitewashed room. Just a quick trip to a cell, a clanging of metal doors and silence. They hadn't even booked him. Rush realized that he was buried, incommunicado. He could rot there for all Hacker cared. They'd hang everything they could on him, rush him through a fast trial and that's the end of Rush Henry.

He lit a cigarette and grinned into the darkness. He didn't feel like grinning, but he forced the smile to his face. It was a morale measure. If he could smile at himself things didn't seem so bad. So he made himself smile at himself. Smile pretty, Mr. Henry.

A half a package of cigarettes later the door opened and a figure entered the half light of the cell. He sat on the single wooden chair that stood opposite the cot. Rush peered at him through the dimness.

"Hello, Max," he said as he recognized his visitor. "What brings you here?"

Carney lit a huge cigar with great deliberation.

"I came here because I'm scared stiff, Henry." He held up a hand to stop Rush from talking. "Let me finish. I know what you're in town for. You want to run me out. I also know that you're not going around knocking off everybody that gets in your way. You don't operate that way. You got too much to lose and the price isn't high enough to hire your gun. Even a five year old ape could tell that that setup in your hotel room was aimed at you and misfired. But it makes a nice frame. I think they could make it stick with a little help from a friendly judge and a packed jury."

"That's all old stuff, Carney," said Rush. "Get to

the new part, about how you're scared stiff."

"Coming up," said Carney. "The only thing left to figure is that somebody else is going around with a fast rod and gunning everybody in sight. The way things are going I figure I'm next. Now I got all kinds of boys working for me, but they're just muscle boys. They do what I tell them and no more. I need somebody to find out who's doing the shooting and stop him before he gets around to me. That's you."

"Me?" asked Rush.

"You. I know you'll run me out of town if you can but I know that you won't gun me down doing it. I'll get you out of this can if you'll find out who's doing the shooting."

"I was working on that when Duffy swallowed the whiskey. I've got a couple of leads. But how are you going to get me out of here?"

Carney laughed.

"I'll tell Hacker to open the door. The rest is up to you. You just walk out."

Rush swung his feet over the edge of the cot.

"You know I'll still run you out of town, Carney," he said.

"Sure. If you can. But if I have the choice I'd rather be here to be run out of town then planted six feet under."

"Okay," said Rush, "tell Hacker to open the door."

An hour later Rush was in his room at the hotel. He had contacted Robin and was waiting for the little man. When he came he had nothing to offer.

"We've checked everybody in the hotel. There's no lead at all. Of course in a good sized hotel like this people can do a lot of wandering around without being seen. It could have been anybody."

"Okay," said Rush. "Keep on it. Maybe somebody'll remember something." He looked at his watch. It was three o'clock. "Damn, I've wasted almost a full day. It's Sunday, too. There's nothing more to do today. I've got to see Prime and Pedrick before tomorrow then I'm going to relax. Tomorrow will be a full day. We've got to win an election tomorrow."

Prime and Pedrick were not available by telephone at any of their usual stands so Rush called Gay. She was both hungry and willing to relax. Rush took her to dinner at a roadhouse several miles out of town. They talked of everything in the world but Forest City and the job Rush was doing there. As they drove back in the cool of evening Rush felt renewed and fresh. He stopped the car in front of Gay's apartment and turned to her.

"You are getting to be a habit I'm going to find it hard to break," he said. "You're good for me."

"That puts me in a class with fresh vegetables, Old Overholt Rye and plenty of sleep. It's very romantic."

"My plans include a large bunch of romance. But the time is not yet ripe. I'm carrying too big a load to give it the attention it deserves."

"Well, don't let it slip your mind at the last minute," said Gay.

"You can count on it," said Rush. "Now, the time has come for me to blow. I have to run down Prime and Pedrick before I get to bed."

He leaned across Gay and opened the door. She stepped out onto the grass parking. Rush slid across the seat and out of the car. He stood for a minute stretching his muscles then he took a step toward Gay. His hand was out reaching for her arm when something tugged at the sleeve of his coat and burned his arm with fiery heat. In the same second a shot rang out from across the street and down the block a hundred feet. In a flash Rush had thrown Gay to the sod and was lying across her. His hand shot to the holster at his shoulder and his gun was out pointing in the direction of the shot. A motor roared and a car leaped away from the curbing, its motor straining at the gears. Rush stood up and looked after it but it was gone before he could even recognize its body type.

He reached down and pulled Gay to her feet.

"Get in the house fast," said Rush. "They may come around the block again and make another pass at me."

Gay's hand went to his sleeve.

"You're hurt," she said in a strained voice.

"Just a scratch. Now get going."

"But your arm—"

"I'll dress it at the hotel. I want you to get out of here."

The urgency in his voice got to her. Reluctantly she left him and entered the apartment house. Rush dove in the car and was instantly in motion. He drove to the hotel and left the car for the doorman to park. He took an elevator to his floor and hurried to his room.

He put his hand on the knob and stopped. It was unlocked and he could hear voices inside. The knob turned under his hand and the door came open. A uniform policeman was standing in the doorway with a gun trained on his stomach.

"Come in, Henry," the cop invited. "Come in with your hands over your head."

Chapter 19

Rush slowly raised his hands over his head and advanced into the room. Inside the room sitting in the easy chair was the plainclothesman who had searched Rush's luggage on his first night in town. He looked at Rush as he came into the room and stood before him.

"Couldn't keep your nose clean, could you?" he asked.

"I didn't know it was dirty," said Rush. "What's up?"

"There's enough up to hang you three times."

"Has Hacker been hitting the pipe again or have you really got something?" asked Rush.

"This time we really got something."

"Could I know what it is?"

"I don't mind telling you," said the plainclothesman. "We got the gun that did the shootings." He shook his head. "An old hand like you leaving a a gun right on top of a closet shelf. You should be ashamed of yourself."

Rush looked at him reflectively.

"I should be," he said, "and I would be if I'd left it there. How'd you happen to look for it?"

"You got a friend that phoned us a hint. We came right over."

"When was this?"

"Early this evening. About seven o'clock."

"Have you checked the gun through ballistics?"

"Check. It fits. It's the gun all right."

"Can I lower my hands and light a cigarette? Your boy seems to know what to do with his gun."

"Lower your hands. I'll light your cigarette." He pulled one from his own package, lit it and handed it to Rush. Rush dragged deeply.

"I don't suppose it occurred to any of the mental giants at headquarters that the gun might be a plant. Especially since someone was nice enough to call in and tell them about it."

The man in the chair grinned.

"You don't suppose Hacker would look an inch further than that gun, do you? It gives him a clean out on all the killings. Hell, he can be a hero." He laughed again. "You should of stood in bed. I told you we didn't like private eyes in this town."

"How do you figure the gun deal?" asked Rush.

"Oh, hell, it's a frame all right. It's a cinch somebody's trying to hang the killings on you. I figured you for them all the time till this came up. Now, I figure it has to be somebody else, unless maybe you're trying a double frame. Putting us on to the gun so it'll look like a frame." He peered closely at Rush. "No, I guess you wouldn't do that. That'd be silly in this town with as much heat as there is on these killings."

"But you've still got to take me in."

"Sure, I'm a cop. I do what I'm told."

"It couldn't be that I forgot to come back to my room tonight. You could wait a while and then call in for instructions."

The man in the chair considered that.

"Well, you'd have to fix Fogarty there. I imagine fifty bucks'd do it."

"I'll make it a hundred. I'm on an expense account."

"That enough, Fogarty?" The uniformed cop nodded.

"You gotta keep your mouth shut though," he said.

"I'll clam up," said the plainclothesman.

"Okay," said Rush, digging for his wallet. "How about you?"

The man in the chair shook his head.

"It's the damndest thing but I just can't make myself take a nickel. I could have gotten well on my job years ago. But I can't make it go down. I guess I'm a softy."

Rush squinted at him.

"What's your name?" he asked.

"Roswell," he said. "Bill Roswell."

"Stick around, Bill," said Rush. "Maybe I can get you well and you won't have any trouble with your conscience. You can even like private eyes if you want to when I get through with this town."

"That'd be very nice. Now scram and go out the back way. I don't want to have to explain how I missed you if half of Forest City see you in the hotel."

Rush left the hotel by the service door at the rear. By back streets and alleys he came to the back door of the Padgett House, Robin's hotel. Through it's service door he entered the hotel and walked up the fire steps to Robin's room. There he did a bit of lock picking of his own and entered the room locking it behind him. He picked up the phone and gave the number of the *Chronicle*. He asked for Bill Prime.

"This is the Chicago Kid," he told Prime.

"Where in hell are you?" asked the editor.

"Where I can't be found," said Rush. "Has anything come in on me from the law?"

"Yeah, they've got a general order out to pick you up on sight. The warning says that you may be armed and to shoot at the first sign of trouble."

"Are you carrying the story?"

"On page five and it sounds like you are a stranger from out of town. No connection with anything else. If anything it sounds like you are a part of the gang war now on in Forest City."

"Good. It'll bring in a thousand votes. How do you figure the story?"

"It's too obvious. But Hacker's calling it hanging evidence."

"Let him. I'll fix his wagon later. I've got a nominee for Chief of Police who'll run him out of town."

"Anybody I know?"

"No. Just an honest cop I ran into in my hotel room."

"What are your plans?" asked Prime.

"The same as before. Look, take notes on this, will you? I've got an idea for an election morning edition."

"Shoot."

"Two column pictures of Gunn, Carver and Hacker on the front page. Then in bold face type print a list of every shooting, every act of violence that happened in the last ten years plus every mistake they've ever made below the pictures. Then in headline type at the bottom of the page say DO YOU WANT THESE MEN TO RUN YOUR TOWN?"

"That's dynamite. They might be able to sue."

"If they lose the election they won't be around long enough to sue. I'll have the new Chief put them in the jug if they even open their mouths. He can dig up enough stuff to send them all over. He's been in the department long enough."

"Okay, I'll take a chance. When you came into the office I told you I'd go all out, but I hope to God you know what you're doing."

"I do. Now, on the back page print a half page

spread of Covington. He's a big, honest, good looking guy. Below his picture print his record. Add
a few of his better campaign promises and in the
smallest type you can find and in one tiny corner.
Say that it's a political advertisement. Bill me for
it. I may even pay you if Covington wins and the
line will put you in the clear."

"Man, you're just taking over my paper, aren't
you?"

"Just for one edition. You can have it back at
noon Tuesday."

"Okay. Will do. If I get shot I'll die knowing I
did my duty."

"Just don't let them see the whites of your eyes,
they may never shoot then."

"How can I get in touch with you?"

"Are you sure your line is clean? No switchboard operator listening?"

"Not a chance. I train my people well."

"Okay, I'm in 823 at the Padgett House."

"How are you registered?"

"I'm not. The room belongs to one of my boys.
A Robin Twist."

"Okay, I'll keep in touch with you. And for
God's sake be careful. Hacker's not fooling."

Robin came in at noon and was not surprised
to find Rush.

"I heard the heat was on and figured that if you

could cop a sneak you'd turn up here. I don't think anybody's made me as belonging to you."

He left with instructions, to round up the boys for a meeting. At four o'clock Matt Pedrick knocked on the door and came in after Rush had surveyed him through the transom.

"Quite a spot you've gotten yourself in, old boy," he said. "I don't suppose you did push those guys off?"

Rush grinned at him.

"You know better than that, Matt. Now, have you got anything Bill can use in his first edition tomorrow morning? We're blasting the lid off of this town. I want him to print everything Patrick Gunn, Mark Carver or Tom Hacker ever did that missed the straight and narrow by even an inch. I want it on that front page if they ever matched coins to see who'd pay for a drink. What have you got?"

"If Bill'll print it I have a lot. I'll dig in my files. One way or another I eventually find out everything that goes on in this town. I've picked up a lot of stuff I've never dared to use before. Maybe I can clean out my files on tomorrow's first edition."

"That should do the job. Here, let's have a slug of Robin's whiskey."

He went to the table and poured whiskey in two glasses. His hand was out holding a glass to Pedrick when the building shook and through the open window the sound of a blast poured into the room. The two men looked at each other and as one man turned and ran to the window. Two blocks away and to their right a column of smoke rose slowly into the air, lazily drifting north on a slight breeze.

"Hell, that could be the *Chronicle* Building," said Pedrick. He dove for the phone but it rang before he could reach it. Rush pushed past him and picked up the receiver.

"Yes," he said.

"Prime here, Rush. I'm afraid your election morning edition is out. Some son of a bitch just dropped a pineapple in the press room. We won't get to press for a couple of days, I'm afraid."

"Any other damage?" asked Rush.

"Not much. It played hell with the presses but outside of a lot of smoke and broken windows that's the damage."

"Okay, we've got to work fast. Get the pics I wanted and all the dope you were going to use. Put them in an envelope and get them over here inside of a half hour. I'll get them printed."

"But how can—"

"Don't ask questions. Get me that dope and have your delivery boys around in the morning. We'll send out an edition of the Chronicle that'll really fix the mob that ran this town. You notice I said, ran. Now get with it."

Rush hung up and turned to Pedrick.

"You heard what happened. Now you get over to the paper and help Bill with the dope. I'll see that it get's printed."

Pedrick shook his head.

"You beat everything I ever saw before. You never give up, do you?"

"Not while I'm on my feet. Get going man. Time's awasting."

When Pedrick had gone Rush sat at the writing desk and covered several sheets of Padgett House stationery with closely written instructions. An hour later the envelope came from Prime and almost simultaneously Robin Twist returned to his room.

Rush put his own sheets of paper in the envelope with Prime's material and handed it to Robin. From his wallet he took some money.

"Take this to Pappy Daley in Chicago. Tell him to print it exactly as I've written it there. You can charter a plane at the airport. I'll call Pappy and have the press rooms ready. It'll take you two hours to get there and two hours back with an hour and a half to and from the airports. That gives Pappy about three hours to print. You should get back here by three or three-thirty at the latest. Now, blow, son. You're carrying the ball for the next nine or ten hours."

Robin left without a single question. Important

things such as his life had depended on Rush being right in the past and Rush had never been wrong. He had gotten out of the habit of asking questions of Rush.

Chapter 20

Pappy Daley phoned Rush at midnight that Robin was on his way. Rush called Prime to send a truck to the airport. Then he left the hotel the way he had come and by more back streets and alleys made his way to the back door of the *Chronicle*. He slipped inside without having been noticed by a single person. He found Bill Prime in his office.

"Hello, fugitive," said Prime. "Did anyone see you come in here? I'd hate to have Hacker close my paper up because I was an accessory after some fact or other."

"I'm clean," said Rush. He looked at his watch. "It's two o'clock. Robin should be in within thirty minutes. When will you be ready to deliver?"

"The carrier boys come in at four. The trucks start for the newsstands at five."

"Is everybody all set?"

"They'll be here."

Rush walked down the hall to Pedrick's empty office and appropriated a bottle from his wall bar. He carried it back to Prime's office and poured drinks in spills of copy paper. They smoked for a half hour eyes constantly straying to their watches. Then the phone on Prime's desk rang. He answered it, spoke briefly then handed the phone to Rush.

"Yes," he said.

"Robin here, Rush. Bad news."

Rush held the mouthpiece away from him for a moment looking at it. Then he put it back to his ear.

"Bushwacked?" he asked.

"Bad. They shot the driver and we bounced off a tree. There must have been ten of them in a truck and two cars. I played dead till they unloaded the truck then I tried to catch numbers on the cars but they had them covered. No go. I hit for a phone and here I am."

"Come on in to the *Chronicle* office," said Rush. "Don't feel bad. It was my fault. I should have figured on a leak somewhere and had you covered. See you in a little while."

Rush cradled the phone and looked across at Prime.

"And I thought I was smart," he said bitterly.

"Don't let it get you. It was a damn near miss."

"Miss, hell. It drops the bottom out of a couple of weeks' work. It puts everybody who's been working with me on a spot. It loses the election for old Covington." He stopped and snapped his fingers. "How about the radio station? Can we buy some time or something?"

Prime shook his head.

"The Federal Communication Commission has put the fear of God into them. They don't handle anything that isn't straight news. They wouldn't touch it yet. It smells of politics."

"That does it then. We can just sit and cross our fingers and hope Covington makes it anyway."

Rush didn't sound as though he had much faith in the hope.

The phone rang again. Rush reached for it. It was Smoky.

"Lose something, chief?" he asked.

"Yeah, thirty thousand newspapers."

"They looked like they might be yours so I followed them."

Again Rush looked at the phone.

"Smoky," he said. "Do you know where those papers are?"

"Sure. I thought they might need a convoy so I followed them from the airport. They are now in a basement about three blocks from you. At least they were five minutes ago when I left to phone."

"Where are you?"

"In a cigar store corner of Eighth and Center."

"Stay right there. I'll be there with a truck in two minutes."

He hung up the phone and turned to Prime.

"Have you any huskies in the pressroom?"

"We don't have a pressroom anymore, remember. But I've got some pretty tough truck drivers and they should be here now."

Five minutes later one truck carrying Rush and six truck drivers armed with clubs picked up Smoky at the corner of Eighth and Center. He directed them south on Eighth Street for a block and a half. There he called for silence, lights out and a slow left turn. The truck rolled to a stop in the canyon formed by the rear walls of buildings on either side.

Smoky led the way in single file along one of the buildings. They came to a freight door set in the wall with its bottom at bed level with the truck.

"They're in there, Rush."

"Okay. Wait here."

Rush took a pencil flashlight from his pocket and a gun from his shoulder holster. He crept ahead to the corner of the building and turned into a narrow passageway between two buildings. As he walked he played his flashlight on the wall of the building to his left. His light caught the corner of a window sill ten or fifteen feet above the level of the passageway. It was well out of hand reach. He surveyed the buildings for an instant, then, in the manner of a mountain climber in a crevice, placed his back against one building and his feet against the other and began to wedge his way up the walls of the narrow passageway. In a minute or two he was level with the window. Then wedging his feet more securely he reached across with the butt of his gun and knocked out a square of glass. Through the opening he unlatched the window and in a second or two was inside the building.

He stood for a moment absolutely still, listening. No sound came for five seconds. Then from below in the building somewhere a whisper of an echo of voices. Rush slowly relaxed his tense listening. Lightly, on the balls of his feet, a pencil of light flashing for a second now and then, he moved toward the sound of the voices. They came louder as he turned a corner and saw in a brief flash of light the yawning depths of a stairwell. Cautiously, stepping only on the sides of the steps he descended. At the bottom he looked left and right. To his right a line of yellow light shone under a door. He walked to it and put his hand on the knob. With infinite slowness and care he tried the knob. When it had turned full turn he pulled it a fraction of an inch toward him. The door was not locked. Then without hesitation he flung the door open and walked into the room, his gun fanning the room in front of him.

Two men, on either side of a rickety table sat dealing rubbery cards. Their faces, turned to meet Rush, were studies in arrested emotions. Rush wasted no words.

"Open the freight door," he ordered.

They continued to stare at him. His finger tightened on the trigger and a bullet tore through the top of the table spattering cards on the floor.

"Open the freight door," he said.

In slow motion, sidling around Rush, the two men left the room. Behind them Rush followed with his gun in hand and the flashlight trained on their backs. A minute later the door was open and Smoky led the truck drivers into the building.

They found the papers still in their original bundles stacked in a corner fifteen feet from the door. Rush looked at his watch.

"It's three forty-five. The carriers will be ready for them in fifteen minutes. Get them to the *Chronicle* building fast. I want to look around here for a minute."

The truck drivers took the two men with them and left. Smoky stayed behind with Rush. They found lights and began a search of the building. Smoky found steps to the basement and went on a side trip alone. Rush was working toward the front of the building when he heard Smoky calling. He went to the steps and down into the basement. In a far corner behind a mammoth heating plant Smoky was on one knee bent over what looked like a pile of rags. He looked over his shoulder at Rush.

"I just found ten thousand votes," he said. "Somebody did in our Mr. Carney."

Rush walked over to the body and stood looking down at it.

"That's all of them," he said. "A clean sweep. Marr, Sully, and now Carney. If X did all this he was wasting his time hiring me. He's cleaned up his city by a process of elimination."

He shook his head and turned away.

"Let's get out of here, Smoky. I'm getting sick of looking at stiffs. I want a drink."

He got it from the bottle he had extracted from Pedrick's bar. He drank straight from the neck swallowing until the warmth struck deep and started melting the cold greasy ball in the pit of his stomach. Bill Prime came back into the office.

"I just talked to the newsroom at the radio station. They'll carry Carney's death on all newscasts. He'll get full coverage. It should give Covington a landslide."

"Yeah," said Rush and drank again from the bottle.

"Isn't it a little early to celebrate?" asked Prime. "The votes aren't counted yet."

"I'm not celebrating. I'm trying to drown a guilty conscience."

Prime stared at him.

"What are you doing with a guilty conscience?" he asked.

"I think I could have stopped all this killing. Oh, not right away, but soon. I should have figured the whole thing at the beginning. I should have seen through X long ago."

"You know who X is?"

Rush nodded.

"I think so. I'm not sure of anything right now. But there's only one way it could be."

"Then what are you waiting for? Go get him."

Rush shook his head.

"You forget I'm wanted by the cops. I have to wait till Covington is elected and installs a new police chief before I make a move. It's all right. He's knocked off everybody who was in his way. There's plenty of time." His voice stopped abruptly on the last word. "The hell there is."

He grabbed the telephone and dialed a number.

"Is Bill Roswell around the station?" he asked when he got his number.

"Just came in. Here he is."

Roswell's voice said, "Hello."

"This is the ex-resident of 715 at the hotel. Catch?"

"Catch," said Roswell.

"Can you find a half dozen honest cops, at least honest enough to do a job if they get paid for it?"

"Can do. Six but no more."

"Okay. Get them. Offer them fifty bucks for the night. Put them around W. C. Covington. If anybody looks cross-eyed in his direction for twenty-four hours, pick them up and bury them somewhere till I can get to them."

"Is that gun going off again?"

"It'll try, if I figure things right."

"We'll cover him like a blanket."

"Call me through the paper if anything happens."

He hung up then.

"Who was that?" asked Prime.

"Your next Chief of Police, if I have anything to say about it."

"Isn't there something you forgot?" asked Prime.

"What?" asked Rush.

"On the face of it you could use about six cops yourself. Your Mr. X might decide to dispense with your services the easiest way."

"Let him try. It'll save me the trouble of going after him."

Rush got up then and walked to the door. With his hand outstretched for the knob he turned and with that same hand swept up the unfinished bottle of whiskey he had taken from Pedrick's bar.

"I'm going to bed," he said. "After I've gone call Gay Wimberly and tell her I'm in hiding. That I'm okay but I can't see her till tomorrow night." He looked at his watch. Six o'clock. "Hell, wait till daylight to call her and tell her I'll see her tonight."

He walked to the door and this time he turned the knob and left.

Chapter 21

Four hours' sleep took Rush to ten-thirty. He awoke and turned on the radio at his bedside. Barry Cameron was in the process of despairing of ever keeping the love of his wife, Anna. He tried another station and got household hints. The local station had music. He turned the radio off and scowled at the ceiling. There'd be nothing on the wireless now, anyway: No returns would be in till late afternoon at the earliest. He wondered where Robin had spent the night. The bed beside him was unslept on. Robin answered his question by coming in dead tired.

"Well, I finally delivered that ball I was running with," he said.

"What have you been doing all night?" asked Rush.

"Delivering papers. I took Prime's car and roamed the streets. I was afraid there might be some trouble and I kept track of as much as I could but nothing happened."

"I wonder what happened to X. It's not like him not to make another stab at stopping delivery of those papers."

"I've been thinking about that," said Robin. "I've got a hunch that X had practically no organization—just a few free lancers he picked up. When he ran out of helpers he was lost."

Rush nodded.

"Could be. With Sully, Marr and Carney out of the way he wouldn't need much of a mob to move in, if that's what he has in mind."

"He'd need a mayor, though, and a chief of police."

"I think that's where I lost X. He wanted the big boys out of the way and hoped to hang them on me. But he didn't expect Pat Gunn to lose the election. By the way, any word?"

"Prime's got a man at every poll. He's had a few phone calls and it looks like a landslide for Covington. Everybody's voting for him."

Rush reached for the telephone and asked for Covington's number.

Covington himself answered the phone.

"It looks like you're in, Mr. Covington," said Rush.

"Thanks to you," said Covington. "By the way, I'm not a coward, really, but after the other day I'm a little jumpy. I may be mistaken but I think there is somebody watching this house. I see the same men passing by every so often."

"They'd better be passing by every so often. They're your bodyguard. The only six honest cops in town are taking care of you. Your new Chief of Police is in charge of them."

"My new what?"

"Your new Chief of Police. I'll introduce you later. He doesn't even know it himself."

"You're an amazing person, Henry."

"I often think so myself. I'll see you this afternoon, Mayor."

Rush hung up then and turned back to Robin.

"Round up Merwin and Smoky. Make a round of the polling places and try and figure out what's happening for sure. Then hit the dives. I want to know what the trouble boys are thinking. They haven't anybody to turn to that I know of, but if there is anybody, or they're considering putting anyone up for boss, I want to know it before it happens."

Robin left then and Rush called Gay.

"Henry?" she said. "The name is familiar. Isn't some female always calling you on the radio? Oh, no—that's Henry Aldrich. You must be someone else."

"You'd better get new writers—your material is beginning to smell. Besides, I'm too tired and too busy to make funny."

"Okay, chief, what's on your mind. And may I add that it's nice to hear from you at last? You are alive, aren't you?"

"It's only an unconfirmed rumor at present. What I'd like is to know what the chances are of finding you alone with a very tall, very dark drink, a deep soft davenport and absolute quiet about ten o'clock tonight."

"The chances are about a hundred to one for. This, I take it, is a proposition?"

"This could develop into anything. It depends on what happens to me between now and ten."

"Make an effort to bring all of yourself, won't you? I want you all in one piece."

"I'll bring everything that counts."

"That'll be very nice of you, I'm sure." Her voice changed timbre. "Is it all over, Rush?"

"Almost, Gay. There's just a little left to clean up."

"Be careful, Rush. I'm not joking now, you know."

"I know. Good-bye, Gay."

"Good-bye, Rush."

Rush had lunch in Robin's room. From time to time during the early afternoon the phone rang and Prime or Robin would report on the election. By four o'clock it was all over but the final count. Covington was in by a landslide. Gunn had already issued a statement conceding. Robin called at four-ten.

"We've cased most of the spots, Rush. The word for what we find is confusion. Nobody knows who's going to do what or to whom. I think if one of them had the guts to step out and say I'm boss he could make it stick, but so far nobody's had the guts.

Anyway nobody's made a move yet."

"I'm going to move fast before anyone gets the idea and the guts at the same time. Get my car from the lot and meet me at the service entrance in the alley behind the hotel. I'll be there in ten minutes."

Fifteen minutes later Robin was steering the car through the residential district toward the home of W. C. Covington. He braked it to a stop at the curb exactly at four-thirty. Rush got out of the car and headed up the flagged path to the door. He got about ten steps. A man stepped out from behind a low pine tree and stood in his way. One hand remained suggestively in the man's pocket.

"Not today, bud," he said. "No visitors."

"Is Bill Roswell around?" asked Rush.

"Could be. Why?"

"Let's go see him."

"In front of me. He's around on the north side of the house. Keep your hands at your side and walk slowly."

Rush followed directions till they came to another tree. Just beyond was a clump of bushes. Roswell stepped out from behind the bushes.

"I thought you'd be around," he said. "Okay, Mart. You can go back in front. Watch it." He turned back to Rush. "Want to see the Mayor?"

"Right," said Rush. "So do you. Come on in with me."

"What for? I should stay out here."

"We'll be able to cover him from in there. I want you to meet him."

They walked around to the front of the house and rang the bell. A maid took them to Covington in his study. Covington came around the end of his desk to shake hands with Rush. He extended his hand to Roswell at Rush's introduction.

"Now, Mr. Covington, can I monopolize the conversation for a minute? There is something that has to be done immediately or you'll have the same problem on your hands you've always had."

"What do we have to do in such a hurry?" asked Covington.

"You have to appoint a new Chief of Police and get him to work tonight."

"But, I can't do that. The election isn't official till the ballots are counted."

"To hell with the ballots. You know and I know that you're in. So start acting like a mayor. Look, Mr. Covington. When Sully, Marr and Carney died they left a large organization behind them. That organization is flopping around now looking for a new head. Sooner or later somebody's going to rocognize the vacuum that exists where those three were and move in. If he makes it stick you've got twice the job on your hands when it comes to cleaning up your town. If you move now, you can do it over-night."

"That's fine, Henry. But where am I going to find men I can trust to do the job? That's going to take time."

"It's going to take about thirty seconds. Here's your new Chief of Police." He turned to Roswell who had been silent during the conversation. Now he looked at Rush as though he had suddenly gone out of his mind.

"Me?" he said.

"You're honest, aren't you?"

"Reasonably, but—"

"Save it," said Rush. "This is no time for doubts. Mr. Covington, Bill is honest. I know. He's got six men he can guarantee as being honest guarding your house. There must be others in the department. How about it, Bill?"

"There are dozens but they never dared let anybody know they might be honest. They needed their jobs so they did what they were told."

"Okay, there's your police force."

"Sure. But what do I do?"

"You have the time of your life. I want you to organize as many squads as you can muster. Send them to every dive in town and tell everybody who can't show a legitimate job that he's due out of town in twelve hours or he goes in the jug for vagrancy. Tell them the town's got religion and they're out. Put a padlock on the door of every gambling joint and horse book in town. Then tell the girls that it's all over now. Give them twenty-four hours to get out of town. Tomorrow morning send your squads out again and start hauling them in. Keep them on bread and water for a couple of days and then haul them to the city limits and start them walking. They'll get the idea right away. I've got some boys that nobody knows circulating downtown now. If anybody starts getting ideas they'll get the word. I'll pass it on to you and you pick up any would-be big shots before they get off first base. It's simple. By the time it's all over the votes will be counted and it'll be official. In the meantime you'll have prevented a tough situation from developing and Covington can start his term with a nice clean city and a reputation for cutting through red tape when the situation indicates it."

Rush stopped and lit a cigarette. Beside him Roswell drew a deep breath and looked at Covington.

"Do you think we can get away with it, Henry?"

"Of course. Pick up your phone and call the radio station. Issue a statement that Bill is now Chief of Police. Then tell what his orders are and say that he is starting to put them into force tonight. Bill, you go to headquarters and take over Hacker's office. Covington'll give you a letter. If Hacker makes any trouble have your boys throw him in the can. I don't think it'll be tough to dig up a charge. Then call in every cop you can trust and go to work. They ought to enjoy it after kissing the behinds of every tinhorn gambler in town for the past ten years."

"They'll love it," said Bill. He looked again at Covington.

Covington took a deep breath and reached for his telephone. He dialed the number of the radio station.

Ten minutes later Roswall was on his way to the police station. Covington looked troubled.

"I know what's on your mind, Mr. Covington," said Rush. "I'm going to take care of that right away."

"You mean the killer?"

Rush nodded.

"I'm going to bring him in myself."

"Won't you want some help from Roswell?"

"No," said Rush slowly, "this is one I've got to handle myself. It'd be easier with a squad of cops but Bill needs them downtown. Besides, it's really my job. Somebody's paying me ten thousand dollars to do it." He smiled at the irony of that and reached across the desk to shake Covington's hand.

"When this is all over I'll deliver my famous little speech on how much vice is good for a city. You have to expect a little. But if you keep a finger on it, keep the gambling legitimate and small, you won't have any trouble. There'll always be a few women in every town, no matter how clean, that make a living the ancient way. The only thing you can do is keep them clean and unorganized. The big thing, the thing on which all other vice feeds is racketeering—collecting from not only legitimate business men for protection, but preying on their own kind selling protection from the law. That's Bill's job and yours. To see that nobody gets rich for not doing something, something that they should do." Rush grinned at Covington. "Damn if I didn't give the lecture already. Now, if you don't mind, I'll have to leave. I have an appointment with a man named X.

Chapter 22

Fifteen minutes later Rush was talking to Bill Prime. Prime asked the same question Covington had posed.

"Okay, you've got Covington in," he said, "now how about the guy with the loose trigger finger? Where's he?"

"I think I know," said Rush. "I'm almost sure but I need a little help."

"Anything I can give you?"

"No, I think this is more in Matt's line. Is he in his office?"

"I think he's at home. He sent his column down by messenger about three after the election was a cinch. He said he felt a party coming on and wanted to get ready. Something about celebrating the election. He said for you to call him."

"I think I'll go out. I want to talk to him and I don't want to use a phone." Rush got up and moved to the door. "I'll be back sometime. How soon depends on how much good Matt can do me. If I don't report in by midnight put Robin on my tail. He'll find me."

Rush found Pedrick in his study seated behind his desk immersed in the study of several papers spread out before him. He looked up as Rush entered.

"Pour yourself a victory slug, pal," he said motioning to a bottle on a corner of his desk. "You did it and I'll bet you're glad."

Rush poured the drink and toasted Pedrick with a wave of the glass. He drank it and set the glass on the desk.

"I'm afraid I've only got half a victory so far," he said.

Pedrick pushed the papers back and leaned back in his chair.

"Yeah," he said. "I expect that's what you have. Got anything in mind to do about it?"

"I've got a lead," said Rush. "It may take some pressure but I think I can make it come through."

"What have you got?" asked Pedrick.

"You remember I asked you about a guy named Wellwood, a lawyer?"

Pedrick nodded.

"King Wellwood. I wondered what you wanted with him."

"He's my lead. Through a bit of fairly naive trickery I learned that he is the man who hired me to come to Forest City."

Pedrick came forward in his chair.

"King Wellwood!" he exploded. "What in the world would he hire you for?"

"Oh, I'm quite sure he didn't hire me for himself. He hired me for someone else. He hired me for the guy I keep calling X."

Pedrick relaxed back into his chair.

"Are you sure?" he asked.

"It's a cinch," said Rush. "He made the deal all right. The big point is can I get him to tell me who X is. He can hide behind ethics and legal privilege till hell freezes over if he wants to. However, if I can convince him that his client is going around knocking off people sort of ad lib, maybe he'll come through. What do you think?"

Pedrick scratched his head for a moment then let his hand fall into his lap.

"I don't know, Rush. I don't know what King would say. I'm pretty sure he'd be amazed at your story. He couldn't afford to be mixed up in something like that personally. In the first place he's above money and in the second he has an old family name to protect. I'm inclined to believe that he might at least hint a little."

Rush stood up.

"Okay," he said. "That's what I wanted to know. I'll go see him."

"Wait a minute," said Pedrick. "Sit down."

Rush came back and stood behind his chair. Pedrick looked up at him with a friendly smile.

"Is it really necessary to see Wellwood, Rush?"

Rush shook his head.

"Not really," he said. "I just need a little confirmation."

Pedrick nodded with a satisfied air as though something he had predicted had happened.

"I thought you had it pretty well taped. I guess I'll have to ask you to put up your hands."

Pedrick's hands came up from his lap. In his right hand was a .45 service revolver. Rush smiled slowly and raised his hands above his shoulders.

"Sorry, old boy," said Pedrick. "I hate to do this." He sounded very truthful. "I was afraid of it all the time. I thought maybe I could handle you at first but when I got to know you I knew it would end this way."

"What way is that, Matt?" asked Rush.

"Why, nobody hates the melodramatic more than I do, but I'm afraid you're for it. There's no other way out."

"The only trouble is that you can't cover this one like you did the others, Matt. A lot of people know I'm here and a lot of others know of my lead to King Wellwood. They'll get around to you sure as hell."

"I've got that figured out. I've decided that you're going to commit suicide. That'll be a tacit admission that you knocked off the other boys. I'll take the credit for driving you to it, of course. I'll say that the gun in your room was a bit of double cover. You put it there and called the cops on the grounds that nobody would believe you were dumb enough to do such a thing. I think I've even got Wellwood figured out. I'll say that you asked me to ask Wellwood to hire you. Your excuse was that a friend of yours lost his shirt gambling in Forest City and you wanted to clean up the town. I'll say that I began to be suspicious of you when the killings started. I finally decided that you wanted to take over the town in place of the men running it. That way my motives become your motives and everything that points at me will point at you."

Rush grinned.

"Very neat," he said. "You might even make it stick. I like that about your motives becoming my motives. Very good. What I can't figure is why you had the motives in the first place. You look like a guy who had everything. What are you missing that you want a town like Forest City?"

"That's a tough question, Rush. I've asked myself often. I think I have it figured out. You remember we talked about life and urges and things. I gave you most of it that night. I came with a built-in urge for power. Under ordinary circumstances I expect I'd have made out by running a business of some kind and bullying my employees, but I was a kind of sickly youth and I got pushed around more than a little. Bullys used to love me. Some of the boys used to work out on me every time things got a little slow. I could have told my dad and he could have stopped it but I swallowed it and waited. It did something to me. It's a funny thing. I know what caused it and I still can't do anything about it."

He reached across the table with his free hand and poured two glasses of whiskey. He drained one and motioned Rush to take the other.

"It's a funny thing," he repeated. "I didn't plan to kill Beau Marr at all. The idea of killing anybody never occurred to me for a minute. Then that night of the party I all at once thought what would happen if he were dead. So I killed him. It's as simple as that. It took almost exactly fifteen minutes. It was easy and, this is the part I'm not sure I understand, it was wonderful. I think it's the feeling of power it gives you. You don't think about right or wrong or justice or retribution. You just decide to kill a man, then you kill him. He's dead. He isn't there any more. And you did it." His voice was serious but without passion. His eyes were level and clear. "Do you understand a little of that, Rush?" For the first time there was a faint trace of emotion in his voice. He wanted Rush to understand.

"I understand all of it, Matt," said Rush slowly. "I think that there isn't a doubt in the world that with my testimony you could win a sanity plea hands down."

"I expect I could. I think I'm quite probably unbalanced although they say you're not insane if you think you are. The trouble is that I know right from wrong. They'd hang me, Rush. No, thanks."

"Okay, then," said Rush. "You'd better forget about killing me and start running. Take my word for it, I'm not going to commit suicide. If you kill me it's going to be quite obvious that it was murder."

Pedrick smiled.

"No, Rush. I'm going to knock you out and heave you over the balcony. I'll say you jumped."

"How are you going to get close enough to knock me out?" asked Rush.

Again Pedrick grinned.

"I don't have to. Kit will take care of that. Now, Kit," he said.

Rush whirled. He caught a flash of white, a blur of motion then something exploded below his ear and he fell like a log. He lay very still on the thick pile rug.

"Is he out?" asked Pedrick.

"I think so. Oh, Matt. I'm afraid."

"Don't be. I have everything figured out. Here, give me his hand. I want his fingerprints on this gun. I'm going to say he held the gun on us until he jumped so we couldn't stop him."

Pedrick knelt beside Rush and picked up a limp hand. He fitted the butt of the gun in Rush's palm and forced the fingers around it. The trigger finger he pushed through the guard. Then he started to push it back. It wouldn't push. The other fingers tightened around the butt.

"Thanks, Matt," said Rush. He sat up with the gun trained on Pedrick. With his free hand he massaged the bump swelling below his left ear. "That's the trouble with amateurs. They always slip on the simplest things. I doubt if it ever comes up again, Matt, but if it does, don't even give a second's warning. When you said 'now, Kit' you gave me enough warning to let me fall with the blow. I admit I could have fallen the wrong way and really caught it but I didn't and all Kit did was graze me. Now, you walk over to that wall and stand facing it with your hands high and flat against the wall. You too, Kit."

Pedrick looked at him strangely.

"You know, Rush, I'm almost glad. Those other guys were fun, but I don't think I'd have enjoyed killing you. I can't remember having liked a man as a man since my father died. But I liked you."

"Thank you, Matt," said Rush. "I liked you, too. I wish you'd told me what you really wanted. I could have gotten you your town and you wouldn't have had to kill anybody. You'd have had to run it by my rules, but it would have been your town. Now, go over to the wall like a good boy. I have to make a call."

"No, Rush," said Matt Pedrick. "I like my prescription for you."

He turned and walked straight to the double doors behind his desk. He opened them and stepped out on to the balcony. Kit screamed.

"Aren't you going to stop him?"

"No," said Rush, "I'm not going to stop him."

"Thanks, Rush," said Pedrick. "Buy the boys in the back room one for me."

He turned and vaulted the railing without a backward glance.

The drink was tall. It was very dark. The davenport was softness itself and there wasn't a sound in the room. It was exactly ten o'clock. The silence lasted as long as the tall, dark drink. Ten minutes. Gay poured another. Still the silence. Finally.

"You're almost unbelievable, Gay. I've been here twenty minutes and you haven't asked a single question."

"I'm not going to. You're here and you're all in one piece. That means two things. That it's all over and that you're all in one piece. What more could a girl ask?"

"Don't you even want to know who did what to who and why?"

"No."

Rush came up from his almost prone position and looked at her.

"You don't?"

"No, I already know."

Rush's jaw dropped a quarter of an inch. Then it snapped shut.

"You called Bill Prime."

"No, Rush. I don't know a thing about what happened really. I just know that you must have caught Matt Pedrick and Kit English."

The jaw drop this time was a full inch. Rush was speechless. Gay smiled at him.

"It's partly a hunch. The other part is that so many things happened to you that shouldn't have happened unless somebody knew what you were up to. The only people that knew were Bill Prime, your boys, Matt Pedrick and me. I counted Bill Prime, your boys and myself out and that left Matt. I had it figured out a week ago but I didn't want to say anything. I know how men are about women."

Rush gazed at her in wonder.

"You," he said, "are wonderful. I only had one thing that you didn't. Kit came to my hotel room and tried to bribe me for some mysterious gent. He wanted to pay me fifteen thousand dollars to get out of town, so she said. I'm pretty sure she also left the poison that killed Duffy."

"So that's what she wanted."

"Huh?" It was all Rush could think of to say.

"I was standing outside the balcony door when she invited herself to your room." Gay frowned suddenly and looked straight into Rush's eyes. "You

www.ingramcontent.com/pod-product-compliance
Lightning Source LLC
Chambersburg PA
CBHW020826260626
47169CB00003B/845